DRAGON'S GAP

LOVE'S IMPULSE

L.M. LACEE

FIN AND JUNE'S STORY

A Novella by L. M. Lacee

BOOKS BY THE SAME AUTHOR:

DRAGON'S GAP: (BOX SET 1 PLUS Novella)
DRAGON'S GAP: (Book 1) Reighn & Sage's Story
DRAGON'S GAP: (Book 2) Sharm & Edith's Story
DRAGON'S GAP (Novella) Love's Catalyst)
DRAGON'S GAP: (Book 3) Storm & Charlie's Story
DRAGON'S GAP: (Book 4) Ash & Olinda's Story
DRAGON'S GAP: (Book 5) Ace & Harper's Story
DRAGON'S GAP (Novella) Love's Impulse THIS BOOK
DRAGON'S GAP: (Book 6) Thorn & Ciana's Story
DRAGON'S GAP: (Book 7) Conor & Ocean's Story

COPYRIGHT
Dragon's Gap: A Novella

Fin and June's Story by L.M. Lacee
Copyright © 2012 L. M. Lacee. All rights reserved.
Published by PrivotelConcepts

TABLE OF CONTENTS

LOVE'S IMPULSE

Fin and June's Story

Authors note:
This Novella is written to coincide with book 5, Ace and Harper's story.

CHAPTER ONE:

June sat in her office and looked around blankly at the walls. She felt like she was living in a surreal nightmare. She did not see the photos of all her nieces and nephews, or the family photos of which there were many. Her attention was taken by the painting of a lone wolf climbing a snow-covered mountain.

The wolf's head hung low, searching for something amidst the snow or maybe it was just exhausted. June would admit she spent time each day wondering which scenario it was, and if there were clues within the painting to tell her. She knew she could ask Harper, but worried she would say it was just a wolf climbing a mountain in the snow. For her that did not work, she needed it to be more. Harper had given her the painting when she had admired it.

She had been forced to wrestle it from Edith, who was positive every piece of art Harper produced was hers. In the past, present or even the future, it all belonged to her gallery. June took great pleasure in making sure Edith knew she was in possession of several pieces Harper had gifted her.

In truth, she saw herself as the wolf in the painting; it was she that was searching for the love she so desperately wanted. She knew if she could shift to her wolf, she would look like that lone wolf pining for her mate. She placed her head in her hands and pulled on the hair at her temples again, asking herself, how was it possible that her mate could just turn up out of the blue and be Ella's uncle, a damn dragon.

Finlay Slorah, a male that took her breath away, the very first ime her wolf scented him, she knew he was her mate. If she was honest with herself, she was not that surprised he was a dragon; it stood to reason she lived at Dragon's Gap and all her friends were all mated to dragons.

What did surprise her, was the male refused to bond with her? He had some weird notion that she needed security, as if bonding with a dragon wasn't security enough.

Sadly for June, before she came here having someone have your back, only occurred because they were ordered to, or she paid dearly for them. Never because they felt you were worthy enough to warrant it, since arriving at Dragon's Gap, she had made friends, true friends who became family. They were people she trusted to have her back, so she had more security than she needed.

The other notion he had was he was supposed to provide a place for them to live? When that was just not true, as she had told him. Sage had told him she had a home already, Reighn had told him Lord Rene` and Lord Andre` gifted her with a property not long after she arrived here. As far as June was concerned, there was no reason they could not live in the house and property she owned. But he just negated her home and would not listen when she tried to tell him she was very happy with her property and did not need some kind of enormous estate. She had invited him numerous times to visit the homestead she lovingly restored. So far, he had declined every offer. June sighed, she would never admit this to him or anyone, but she and her wolf felt rejected with his attitude, she had spent months finding furniture and renovating her home, ready for when she would live there and for some reason, he could not get that.

"Ohh." She groaned and laid her head on her arms as she remembered his other issue, the money. She had a nice tidy bank account, he was immensely wealthy, as most dragons were. She was not concerned about that, in fact she did not care, she was house and land rich, he was cash rich, seemed fair to her but not to dragon Finlay Slorah. There was also the little matter of the major hurdle. Employment, he needed to work; she understood that, but he was working. Unfortunately, he wanted to make sure the job was a good fit for him. Apparently almost three months was not long enough to know, even though he really enjoyed every aspect of his job and was not looking for anything else. He told her the right position made him more worthy, and that was important. How did one fight that, a male's honor was not to be belittled or so Sage and Claire told her and she felt that, she really did, except it was just so unfair?

She wanted a home, cubs eventually, she wanted her mate, damn it! Her wolf was feeling rejected and sadly June was starting to agree with her, their dragon was just not into her.

The male was everything she wanted. *Well... hell,* she nodded to herself. He was what any female would want, tall, buff, *OMG!* Was the male buff, and he packed serious hardware. June felt herself go warm remembering his hard flat stomach and eight pack that was just such a turn on. Well, it turned her on.

Sighing, she stared blankly at the small statue of a female standing with a wolf, her hand on its head, both of them looking into the distance. Harper gave her the statue just before she left she smiled as she remembered sneaking it into her bag so Edith would not see it and glare at them both.

She promised Harper not to say anything to Edith, she did not have the heart to tell her. Edith would see it the first time she entered her office. She was like a heat-seeking missile when it came to art.

June pouted, it was exquisite just like Fin, he was just so handsome, and she wasn't the only one to think so. She had heard there were a few females who thought the same. She was going to have to steer them away from her man, but did he see they were sniffing around him? Her mate was an oblivious male for a hard as nails warrior who was not a babe in the woods.

She was honest enough to admit that fact did please her she did not want any young male who was still out to impress and did not know his own mind. But seriously, Fin was as stubborn as the day was long. He annoyed her to her last nerve.

June would agree that some days she was more wolf than human, and she did take on her wolf's thoughts about her mate.

They conversed, maybe not in words, but their conversation in emotions was very clear, her wolf was pining for her mate; she did not understand human relationship issues. She just wanted her mate, June understood that too.

Which is why finally last night she had given into her wolf's demands and asked Fin when they were going to make this mating happen? He had kissed her and told her he was working on it. Like that meant anything, it was the same answer he had said over the last month.

When he first said it to her, she laughed. She did not laugh so much last night, his evasiveness made her see red. So instead of taking the soft approach, June in fact lost her temper. Telling him to get his act together, and until he did, she would refuse to see him. She had stormed from his apartment, and her last look of him had been him standing in the middle of his lounge with his mouth open in shock.

Her anger carried her all the way to her apartment and through a bath and two glasses of wine. When she finally calmed down enough to think, she did feel bad about issuing an ultimatum to him. Which was not helped by her wolf fretting over her demands well into the morning hours?

Consequentially when she rolled out of bed this morning, she was still tired and hovering close to the days when she used to make decisions she regretted later, and to make the day just that much more perfect. It was family Sunday.

So when she finally arrived for breakfast, dreading having to see Fin after the night before. She heard not from him, but his niece, her friend Ella that Fin had left Dragon's Gap to see some friends he used to work with. It seemed he had known days ago he would have to leave because he told Ella and Verity he would not be home for Sunday family day, but he did not once mention it to her. She was devastated, what more proof did she need, the male did not want her.

Glumly she sat now in her office, having to remain cheerful in front of her family was tiring, she just needed time to collect herself, think clearly before dinner. Depression swamped her, with

Fin going away and not telling her it seemed like a big indicator something was wrong. She could only come to the conclusion it was her. Fin had days to tell her he was going away or to ask her to accompany him was he ashamed of her because she was not a dragon? He never acted like he was, but truth was in the pudding. So Grace would say. Whatever that meant.

Sadly, this weekend sort of said all there was to say about their relationship and June was tired of feeling like a puppet dancing to his tune. Time to woman up and do some thinking and to do that, she needed to get away from here.

She knew Charlie was going to ask Harper to do another sensitive retrieval tonight, but she also knew Reighn had told Sage to make sure Harper stayed home. So she would do the job, if Charlie would let her, sighing she admitted it had been a while since she had been on the road. She drummed her fingers on the desk, having second thoughts. Could she do this? Was she prepared to do this? Maybe she couldn't?

She straightened her shoulders and flicked her hair behind her ears. She could do this, she was a good retriever, and she always brought her people home. She needed to do this, the time away that a retrieval would give her to think would be valuable. If she had to, she would beg Charlie to give her the job.

With the decision made, June ran to her apartment, which thankfully was on the first family floor of the castle. As it was Sunday, the castle was quiet, not much foot traffic to cross paths with her, therefore she did not have to explain where she was going and why. She loved her surrogate family, but they were slightly overprotective at times and for some unknown reason they always looked at her decisions with suspicion. But if she was wily as only a wolf could be, she should be able to slip away without anyone knowing especially. *'Mr Working. On. It, dragon.'*

Angry all over again, June quickly packed her retrieval bag, some things, she realized as she placed spare clothes and ammunition in her pack, one never forgot how to do. She loaded up on her personal weapons and changed into her old outfit of jeans, shirt, combat boots and leather coat.

Ready, she looked around, decided she had forgotten nothing and quietly left her apartment, running down the wide stone stairs, she stashed her gear in a small closet off the landing and walked into the family room; it seemed luck was on her side.

CHAPTER TWO:

C harlie and Harper were together and standing by themselves. June smothered a laugh when they both jumped a little as she stepped up to the two of them and slipped the paper Charlie held from her fingers. "I will go. Reighn has said Harper is not to go out again."

Charlie looked concerned as she whispered. "June that is not a good idea."

Harper agreed saying. "Sage will be unhappy."

June looked at the sisters, knowing she needed to make this sound good or they would foil her plan. "Excuse me, I was with Sage when we first started retrievals and I am quite able to look after myself."

"What will Sage and Fin say?" Charlie asked softly.

June could see Harper looked confused, not realizing as everyone else did that Fin and she were in a courtship of sorts. "Why will they say anything? I am not a young one to be asking permission. I am capable and healthier than Harper. No offense."

"Oh, none taken. Truth is truth." Harper agreed with a grin.

"Charlie, I will get it done. I will make it okay. I promise." June argued, hoping Charlie would not ask Sage's opinion. The last thing she needed was to have Sage demanding to know why she wanted to leave the castle.

Charlie smiled, but it did not reach her eyes, she was unhappy, but in truth she could not say no. June was as far as she knew a very good retriever and as she said, she was no child, plus Harper was hurt more than she was letting on.

June whispered. "Charlie, I need this. I need to go out for a while. I need to clear my head. Please don't make me beg."

"Oh June never. Go… go and stay safe, get dead, and I will kill you myself."

June nodded. "See you in a few days and thank you, Charlie." She hurriedly slipped from the room as both Charlie and Harper watched her go.

She ignored her wolf's sorrowful howl, telling her. *It is what we need to do, to decide what our next step is. Please don't be sad. We will be back.*

Later that night, Fin leaned against the wall outside June's apartment and waited for her to return. He had not attended Sunday family day, opting instead to go and see his old comrades when a message was received three days ago to let him know they wished to return home. His dragon insisted he tell June and even invite her to go with him. But he had been worried, the planet his friends had been stationed on was known as a rogue destination.

Finally, he had convinced his dragon she would be safer at home. So he did not tell her he was going, thinking to spare her feelings about being left behind. Ella would say he decided for her and did not give her enough credit to decide for herself. He sighed as he again shifted trying to get comfortable on the hard floor. Maybe Ella and his dragon were right, maybe he was too protective. June was an intelligent, amusing, gifted female and he was a lucky male to have her or would be if he could only stop pissing her off as he had last night.

His dragon told him. *Because you will not employ the strategy, we agreed on.*

We cannot use that. Our strategy did not take into account shifters. They are all about emotions, not as we had originally thought, dragon rational. Wolves are not dragons, and June is more wolf than human.

So what are our options? Our shadow is becoming restless and annoyed with our delay.

We are not ready.

His dragon went silent with that, and Fin mentally shrugged, maybe courting a female wolf was different from preparing for battle. Maybe not all contingencies could be foreseen, he would think on it. He knew he was right, he had to make sure he was secure, that he and his dragon could keep her safe. It was something he had learned as a young male. His brother had not done enough for his shadow or hatchling, and Ella had grown up without him or her parents. He would never allow that to happen to June or any of his young, if he actually had any.

Where was she?

His dragon murmured. *Maybe she has gone to stay at her home. You are tired, today was harder than you thought it would be. Settling males that have not lived in civilized society for many years was enough to try my patience. Go to bed, if we are not to see our shadow. I do not want to be here, where I can scent her anger and frustration, it adds to mine.*

Sighing, he agreed. *Alright. We will find her tomorrow and take her to lunch.*

His dragon grinned, and Fin could almost feel him drooling.

Hamburgers? I like hamburgers.

Yes, you greedy dragon.

CHAPTER THREE:

F in was annoyed, in fact he was beyond annoyed, he was probably closer to incandescent with rage. He walked into the health center where his niece Ella stood talking to an older male; and waited and paced as he felt his anger reach new heights.

He had just been told when he went to June's office to ask her to lunch that she was not there. It seemed she never came into work today in fact, she was not at the castle or Dragon's Gap. Apparently his shadow left last night to do a retrieval. Fin was here at Ella's place of work because he knew she would know if this was in fact true.

As she flicked worried eyes toward him and then quickly away, he felt his heart sink, she knew his June had left him. His dragon moaned pitifully. *Our fault, we took too long. Wolves are not dragons.*

Shut up! The plan was yours as well.

We are doomed to be alone.

Dear Goddess, what kind of warrior are you?

A LONELY ONE! His dragon roared, almost dropping Fin to his knees.

"Uncle Fin?" Ella said carefully after she had finished talking to the male who with one hesitant look at Fin hurried away. Ella felt a little sorry for her uncle, he looked like his world had been rocked and not in a good way as Edee would say.

When Charlie told her this morning at breakfast, that June had left to go on a retrieval, she wanted to jump up and down with glee. Finally, June was taking a stand but now, looking at her devastated uncle, she was not sure that was the best plan.

She felt her Uncle Fin was being ridiculous; she understood his reasons, as did June. Shoot, everyone did, but there was safe and secure, then there was procrastinating. Her uncle was dithering, as Harper would say, and like June she did not know why? "Ella, I cannot find June."

"She is not here. She left Dragon's Gap."

He felt his lungs squeeze his chest, in fear and pain. He had known she was not here but for Ella to baldly say as much, took his breath away. "Why... why? Would she leave without me knowing?"

"Why would she not?" Ella asked as she led him into an office. Hers, by the scent of it. Fin thought as he paced the small room. "She is my shadow."

"Is she? All indications say you have no claim on her."

Fin growled. "You know I do, we have been in a courtship."

Really, males! Her dragon said. *Why must they complicate everything?* Ella sighed before replying. "You have been in a courtship, June and her wolf have been telling you the courtship was over. They want their mate; you denied her. What did you think was going to happen?"

Fin paced again as he told her. "She understood."

Ella was sure she heard him pouting, trying not to laugh, she said sharply. "No, she did not, do not fool yourself she was patient, she was kind, she did understand. Now she has lost patience, she is no longer willing to be a doormat, and she does not understand. All she knows is her mate has rejected her."

He slumped into a chair, his head on his chest. "I do not know what to do. We, my dragon and I, had a plan?"

Sage strode into the room, she hugged Ella then she stood looking at the male. "Well you better think of something my sister left home, without my knowledge and it is your fault dragon."

Fin stood up fast, his face a mask of shame and pain as Sage asked with annoyance coloring her words. "Ella, how did you find out?"

"Charlie told me this morning when we had breakfast."

"Call her here, for me please."

Ella inwardly grimaced, she knew that tone, it boded ill for the one she was angry with... and Sage was angry. It was easy to tell by the way she spoke in the voice of the Dragon Lady.

"Certainly Dragon Lady."

Sage eyed the male. "Please sit, you and I need to have a discussion." She took the seat next to him. "I am going to tell you a few things about your shadow."

Fin looked at her and said nothing. Sage nodded, *good the male was willing to listen.* "Some of this you may know, some not, there is stuff she will not tell you herself, June was brought up by her grandmother."

Fin nodded. "I know she was a mean, bitter, nasty female who abused my June."

Sage sighed. "Yes, she did, and often. June finally escaped her at thirteen and found a wolf pack, a street pack in New York. Thankfully, they were good to her the Alpha believed all pups should be educated, he did not care if the wolves under him were half or full blood. Believe me that was unusual back then, when June was eighteen, her Alpha was killed in a challenge. The new Alpha was not a progressive thinker like the old Alpha and he hated all half-bloods. Just before the challenge the old Alpha feared for June and the half-bloods under his care. He made her swear if he lost to make sure she took all the half-bloods away and gave her a lot of money and a list of places she could take them to, so they could be safe.

As I said, the old Alpha was defeated, and before the new Alpha established himself and his pack. June did as she promised. I am sure you can imagine he did not like that. He hunted her throughout America for months probably still is for all we know. When she had all those under her care safe, she left and traveled the world doing basically what we do now. Except she took them to my uncle's pack for safety."

"I did not know any of that, she never discusses it."

"No, some of those memories are unkind to her and there are some things she did, that she would rather forget."

"I can understand that."

"I am sure you can. The thing you should know about June is she can become wolf crazy."

"What is this term? I have never heard of it before, have you niece?"

"No, I have not. Is it a disease?" Ella asked Sage as Charlie walked in.

"Hello Sage, Fin, Ella."

"Charlie, we are discussing June." Sage told her as Charlie took a seat, she eyed Sage warily, noticing the tight way she held herself. If she was not mistaken, her Dragon Lady was not pleased.

"I see. I am sorry you disagree with my choice but in truth as a retriever she is first class, and she was capable, but most importantly she was willing."

Fin stood. "She is my shadow; you had no right."

Charlie's eyes went ghost gray as she stood as well. "Stand down dragon Fin or I will put you down."

"You may try Assassin." He growled back at her.

"Stand down, my friend." Storm calmly said as he entered the room.

Fin took a step back and shook his head. "I beg your pardon, my apologies."

"Understandable." Charlie said quietly as Storm nodded.

Sage stood, none were left in any doubt that the Dragon Lady stood before them and she was angry, she pointed to Charlie, and in a voice like ice, she said. "I am very angry with you, there was no way you should have allowed her to leave for whatever reason, without talking to me first especially after the last time she did a retrieval. I know you know what happened that time." Then she pointed at Fin. "You and your plan of courting has done nothing but cause her to feel rejected which has done nothing, other than drag up her parents and grandmothers rejection. You have made her doubt herself, she feels as if she is unworthy of a bond, now your work to convince her otherwise when she returns will be like climbing up a mountain without legs. In fact, that may be easier." She took a breath and said softer but no one left in any doubt how angry y she was.

"Realize I am her sister, so what I am saying now is for your ears only. What June has is not for all to learn about, and it is not a disease, it is something that occurs to wolves that have suffered in their formative years as she did. Wolf crazy, for you who do not know the term, means she will take chances you and I would never think to do. She will not see the perils because she does not want too, she will willing walk into a trap in the belief she will best it or her opponents. Why? Because when she is wolf-crazy she never sees the danger in any situation. If people like us get into trouble or feel outnumbered, we will call for back up, she will not. She would never even think to do so. It is not a flaw and it is not because she has a death wish or does not care. She cares, just not about herself, because she believes she is indestructible she becomes wolf crazy." She looked at Fin and said quietly. "The last time she was truly wolf-crazy was just after we started retrievals she rescued three pups from their abusive father, in the process, she killed fourteen wolves before she came home and she did that by walking into their den knowing she was out numbered, out gunned with no back up. When I asked her why, she would take such a chance. She shrugged and told me she never once stopped to consider they would win. She believed she had right on her side."

Fin and Charlie paled as they stared at each other, Sage told him "Fin, if she allows you another chance, you will need to learn the signs. For now I suggest we all sit back and pray to whoever we believe in, that she will come back alive and whole." She looked at them all and bit out. "I am leaving now, please none of you see me for a day or two, unless it is about June. I am very angry."

Without another word she nodded to Storm and left, taking a visibly upset Ella with her. Charlie, with a kiss for Storm and a small smile to Fin, left after she had made sure Sage was nowhere to be seen. Leaving Fin alone with Storm, with an eye on his shadow Storm said. "You and I at the Broadsword now."

Fin nodded as he followed the male from the room. He was in for a pounding, and sadly on some level he knew he deserved it. Maybe he could get some advice from Storm and Lars after his beating, they had bonded with non-dragons.

His dragon snarled. *Now you ask?*

At least I am asking.

His dragon grumbled. *Still lonely.*

Yeah… Yeah!

CHAPTER FOUR:

The music was divine, heavenly tunes reached out into the night causing the hair on June's arms to rise as she sat in her car. It was impossible not to hear the song carried to her on the breeze and feel anything other than sadness.

It had been three days since she had made her mad dash from Dragon's Gap and Fin. She was on her eighth retrieval, and unfortunately there had not been a day since, that her wolf's pining did not make her feel sad. She was no closer to an answer to the problem of Fin. Although she hoped by being out of reach, he may have thought on her last words to him and come to the same conclusion she had. They needed to be together now.

As she listened to the song, she could not help the tears fill her eyes, and wondered who sang with so much heart rendering sorrow. Two rings on her phone let her know her passengers were about to arrive, wiping any tears that may have escaped away she started the car and unlocked the doors. Listening to the last notes of the song fade away under the purr of the finely tuned engine she felt regret as sad as it was, it was also hauntingly beautiful.

Within minutes, her front and back seats were filled with females that sadly brought with them the familiar scent of fear and desperation. When she heard the last door close, she put the car in gear and reluctantly drove slowly from the small town. Knowing she would never be this way again and would be unlikely to hear such beauty again in her lifetime. Sadness washed through her to mix with the fear and anguish residing in the car.

Carefully, she let only her eyes travel over the occupants of her vehicle and was not surprised to see the haunted faces of seven undernourished females and their small children. It had been that sort of town. Even with the beautiful music, there had been an undercurrent of violence and fear in the air that itched at June's nerves. She was relieved to be leaving.

A voice whispered from the darkness. "We are grateful for the ride."

June smiled, and it showed in her voice as she answered.

"No problem, you are not the first we have taken from around here tonight, and as far as I know you will not be the last. All who need to leave, will do so before morning."

"That is a relief, it as a place of horror that I hope we can put behind us." Said another more mature female voice.

June told them. "Where you are going, there are people who can help with that, they are good people. I know it is hard to believe there are places and people who are kind and loving to our kind."

The same voice came from the back seat. "That is what the tigers told us. Sad to say, there were some of us who did not believe them, until tonight when you and your vehicles all arrived."

June nodded. "Yeah, we get that a lot; it is something we have come to terms with. Oh, by the way, who was that playing and singing in the bar?"

There was silence until a young female squashed in the front seat by the door answered. "There was no music or singing in the bar, just the typical fighting."

June jerked the steering wheel. She had not imagined hearing the music or the haunting voice singing. To cover her lapse in concentration she said. "Sorry, bump in the road. Well, it must have been a radio."

They drove so long her passengers finally dropped into an uneasy sleep. When she saw they were really asleep, she messaged her coordinates and a large oval filled with light opened on the road in front of her vehicle. She drove through the silver doorway, a portal was the quickest way to the drop off point. She had discovered over the last three days things had really changed since she had done retrievals.

A bus sat on the side of the road, with a tables and chairs set up under an awning where medical personal were waiting. She must be one of the first cars to arrive she slowed when she recognized one of the figures who detached herself from a table. Faeries, dragons, and shifters streamed out from the darkened bus when her car halted.

June gently woke her passengers. "Ladies, we are here, this is the next step on your road to a new life, these shifters and others will see you to Dragon's Gap. Remember you are now safe."

There were several quiet thank you's, as the doors opened and arms reached for young and adults alike. Soon her car was empty with a tap on her roof she pulled her vehicle around the bus and parked as she saw the headlights of another vehicle come through the re-opened portal.

Getting out, she reached for the cup of coffee held out to her by the female dragon. "Ella, how are you?"

"I am good, you?"

"Good. Sore, a little too much sitting. I need to be running around the castle. I miss my office."

Ella laughed as she asked. "This is your last run, so I was told."

"Gordon said that, right?"

"Yep."

"He told me the same thing this morning."

Ella blurted out. "Fin and I have talked?"

"Oh really?"

"Yes, we all have talked, Storm and Lars have talked. The only ones I think to not have talked to him are Keeper and Reighn."

"Oh dear, that does not sound good."

"So, I ask my friend. Why are you here?"

June sighed. "Your uncle will not commit. My wolf and I got tired of waiting. Wolves or shifters do not like uncertainty in their mates." She looked down into her coffee and admitted softly. "I didn't know what to do. So I ran."

Ella snorted. "He is an ass! He has been haunting Charlie's office every day, driving her mad wanting to know where you are, when you will return. She won't tell him, which ignites his temper."

"I am sorry." June mumbled feeling her and her wolfs sadness at Fin being upset.

"I am not. He is I repeat, an ass!"

June sipped her coffee and smiled at the feisty dragon, then said. "You know, you sound like Edith?" Before Ella could retort, she asked her. "So why are you here? You normally don't come out. Is Keeper with you?"

"No, he was held up in town. I just wanted to make sure you were okay. You are my friend and soon to be my auntie."

"See that is just mean... right there." June growled as Ella laughed. She looked June over. "You look tired."

"I am."

"Are you returning with us?"

"No, I have to go do something."

"Another pick up?"

"Yeah, something like that."

"Would you like company?"

June looked up at the Dragon. "Thank you no. Ella, I will be fine."

"You say that, but you were hurt last time. Sage and Claire have not forgotten and will be annoyed if you get yourself hurt again. Fin will be obnoxious to live with and a certain dragon will roar which upsets his shadow. Who is, as we all know, with hatchlings? And Edith is eyeing the art in your office?"

June laughed then quietly stated. "And yet I am still going." She finished her coffee, and Ella handed her a travel mug with more. June smiled at the dragon. "Thanks mom, see you soon."

"You have a mean streak, wolf. Just you keep safe. I cannot listen to another dragon roaring. I am thinking Uncle Fin will be loud."

June laughed and waved to Ella as she jumped back into the car. She stuck her head out the window and called. "Tell that female to keep her sticky fingers away from my treasures."

Ella laugh, as she watched the taillights of Junes car be swallowed up by the portal, sighing she went to help the new arrivals.

A minute later June was through the portal and back on the

road outside the town she had left only a little while ago. She wound the window down and sure enough the music with the haunting song filled her ears. She drove, almost mesmerized by the tune, toward a mountain range. Miles from the town, or in fact anywhere. With no moon the road was dark, which is why they had done the pickups tonight, undercover of a black sky.

CHAPTER FIVE:

After driving for an hour or more, she pulled off the one lane dirt road into a small parking lot hidden behind a line of trees.

She sat and listened to the engine tick over and looked out the window, seeing shapes in the distance. Mountains, she thought, and trees, lots of trees, some kind of forest. It was so quiet and very still, as though the air forgot to move. She could hear nothing, but she knew something was out there, her wolf was alert and watching.

Taking a deep breath, she could feel eyes on her already, but from what or whom was something she and her wolf could not detect, she decided to wait another five minutes, before she chanced leaving the relative safety of her vehicle. At some point, she would find out who or what was watching and waiting for her but until they revealed themselves, she had something to find.

Decision made, she got out of her vehicle, stretched out cramped muscles and shrugged into her coat, placing her backpack on. She had stuffed it with the normal emergency gear all retrievers carried, thermal blanket, first-aid kit, flares and a sat phone, food and water. She hefted it high on her back as she looked up into the mountains. Then she did as she had been taught, she checked her weapons and realized she could see better now; it appeared her wolf had come on board and added her sight to hers.

Closing the door, she covertly activated her alarms and deterrents, if anyone wanted to tamper with her car, they would end up passed out she knew from experience Sage's spells were a bitch. With a grin she picked out a marker in the distance; as it happened it was a tall tree with large, wide branches. Starting her hike, she hoped to make good time and figured it would take her ten minutes to reach her target, the terrain was inclined but easy to traverse.

Once she reached the tree, she could hear the song again; it was clearer she could almost make out words but the music was so faint it was barely audible. She turned to the right, and the song faded; she turned to the left, and it was louder. She again picked out a landmark to the left and started her trek; it was becoming steeper, and she was having to climb a little now. But it was not impossible, she knew she would be feeling it in her calves tomorrow. The music and song were her guide, following where it led, traveling over rough ground, climbing rocks. Forever climbing higher up the mountain.

An hour after arriving at the car park, June stopped to drink from another one of her bottles and turned her head both ways only to realize the music was gone, although the feeling of being watched was still there. Now only the song remained she still could not hear the words they were just out of her range of hearing, it was as though she was feeling the song not actually hearing it. When she knew which direction to go in, she walked for another ten or fifteen minutes until she came to an entrance of a cave.

Turning on her torch she shone it down the tunnel which thankfully was head height, maybe five or six inches taller than her and about ten feet long. It looked like it opened into a cavern; she took a gun out, and taking a deep breath, muttered.

"In for a penny, in for a pound." She scratched her head and wondered. *Where do I get all these sayings from and what the hell is a pound?*

Moving slowly and cautiously along the narrow tunnel, she eventually came to a relatively large cavern. It was at least as big as a small house, she peeked around the edge of the cave wall and spied a ledge about chest height toward the back half of the cave. She shone her torch and saw a female, and in her arms were cradled two small bundles. June rushed to her, shrugging out of her backpack as she went, the female smiled as she said. "You heard our song?"

"I did."

"I was so worried no one would. You are Fae?"

June grimaced. "No, sorry, I am half-wolf. What happened to you?"

She sobbed. "They came in the night and killed my light. I ran, but the babes wanted to be born. They are early by three weeks, I have given them our light, my males and mine; they will survive. Please take them and keep them safe."

June said. "My name is June Bradly. What is your name?"

"The babies and I called for you, and you heard from all the millions on our world, you heard our song." She sobbed softly as she looked down at her babies.

June wiped the sweat from the females face and told her again. "I am not fae."

Without looking at her, the female mumbled weakly. "It matters not, they chose you."

She offered her a drink which she refused with a smile. June was positive she was fading away as she wiped her face again she felt a tingle on her hands, quietly she said. "Hush now, I will take them to Dragon's Gap, please what is your name?"

She sighed. "Everything you wish to know is on that." She weakly pointed with her chin to a slip of paper that lay on the stone next to her hand. June picked it up and put it in the side pocket of her pack as the female told her. "We were on our way there, they say it is a safe place."

June nodded. "It is, my family make it so."

"Oh how fortuitous, that you were the one to come."

"Isn't it, though?" June said with a smile for the ethereal female who she realized was not faerie as she first thought, "Are you an Elf?"

"No Pixie. The girl's father was a faerie."

"Is there someone for me to contact, for the babies on your behalf?

"No dear one, they will be yours to hold, yours to love and yours to keep safe. Your mate will care for them, hold them safe, he is a good male. I see you as a family, my gifts to you are truly blessed."

June stilled, her body just stopped moving as her mind blanked of all thought as she watched the female just stopped kiss each babies small forehead and fade from the cave.

"Holy shit... I... I..." She took a breath. "Okay, I can do this. So little ones, for better or worse, you called for me, why, only you know. I really hope she was correct, and Fin is going to be your new daddy, because we are going to need all the help, we can get. Now just give me a minute here to sort some things out."

With that she emptied out her backpack, lined it with the thermal blanket and tucked both tiny wrapped bodies within. She looked at each baby who had bright green eyes that open and closed slowly, she mumbled still trying to process what had just happened as she noticed the soft cotton candy pink hair. "Look my wolf, isn't this amazing we have young?"

Her wolf sent her the emotion of happiness and danger it was a heady combination which had her reeling on top of everything she felt her body tremble and heaved in several deep breaths letting the sensation wash over her.

"You are right my friend we still have to get out of here. I get the feeling the people who took these little one's parents, are not going to give up too easily." She kissed both of the baby's heads much as the pixie had done, then murmured. "Well, my pups, we are to leave this haven and go meet your new family, so I need you to just stay in here and remain quiet."

She was slightly amazed at how quiet they were, maybe she thought half-elf and faerie babies were quiet. She would ask Elijah and Scarlett. Right now she had other things to worry about. She could feel the danger her wolf warned her about at her back and knew time and her luck was at an end. Now came the running and shooting stage of this rescue. She quickly zipped the pack almost closed and looped the straps over her shoulders, so the bag rested on her chest.

With some acrobatic twisting and turning as well as an almost dislocated shoulder, she finally got the chest straps to snap closed across her back. Secured, she filled her hands with her pistols.

There were another two guns on her hips, as well as two more strapped to her thighs, easy to reach and fast to draw. Her pockets were filled with more clips of ammunition.

Leaving her torch off, she eased down the tunnel, when she was feet from the entrance. She leaned her back against the rock wall and took in several breaths, her wolf gave her the sensation of sniffing, which June did, drawing in the air and scenting the unwashed stench from the two males just outside the cave saving her and the baby's lives.

She pulled away from the wall and turned so she was facing toward the cavern, thankfully, her coat was reinforced so walking, or in her case running backward to the opening of the cave, would protect her body and the babies at least that was the theory. She just crossed her fingers and believed it would work. Taking several deep breaths and saying a prayer for luck, she ran backward, toward the cave entrance.

When she broke clear from the opening as swords swept across her back, cutting the material of her coat, she did not stop moving and passed both attackers firing, her bullets and finding purchase. One attacker was shot in the throat and face, the other in the head and chest twice. She whirled around and just missed a throat cut of her own, she repeatedly shot the male in the face and chest as he fell backward.

She dropped another male with two bullets to his heart as he rushed her from her right side. Another male fired two shots into her body before she could move out of the way. Luckily her coats protection stopped one, the other grazed her ribs where her coat was flung wide. She swore and emptied the remainder of her clip into him.

Hastily she buttoned her coat over the pack, then swapped out her guns and ran, shooting both guns continuously. Unfortunately, running and shooting is never a good plan, especially in the dark and on a mountain. Trees tended to hinder visibility and brush and roots had a way of tripping or making her stumble, her aim was off, and her guns were basically ineffective.

This did not hinder the attackers as she was attacked by two more assailants hidden in the brush, who rose as she ran pass. Lashing her with their swords, slicing shallow cuts along her g her jean-clad legs. Her arms were covered in the armor lining of her leather coat, so she only received superficial cuts to them. The back of her coat which had been sliced twice already was open to their swords, and as much protection as her jeans and coat provided her, she still bled. Thankfully, the males were not well versed in the use of the weapon, or she was just too fast.

She shot and killed at least one more male, but missed others and kept on running using the trees for cover when she could and when she couldn't. She ran faster around the trees, hoping to use them for deflection. She finally heard shots ring out behind her and smiled she had wondered when they would bring guns to the party.

Several shots 'thunked' into the trees as she passed them, the first ones were wide of where she was, but luck was on their side. All of a sudden she felt the impact of several bullets hit her coat, which propelled her forward on to her hands with the strength of her wolf, she managed to push herself upright and forward, saving her life. The bullet that entered through an opening in her coat would have hit her spine, instead of embedding itself in her shoulder.

She heard yelling as she ran, suddenly the guns stopped shooting and as she listened, a male yelled that guns were not to be used. June thought it was a strange thing to say it was a shame no one told her that before this started, sadly for them, she only came with guns.

Smiling, she ran a little faster until she sniffed out a hollowed out tree behind a screen of bushes. She lay on her back and wiggled under the brush, hoping she did not disturb the dirt too much or leave a trail of blood behind giving away her position. She managed to squirm around enough that she was able to sit with her back in the hole of the tree, looking outward. Leaning her head back against the tree's damp bark and taking in breaths of crisp mountain air. She gave herself a few minutes to settle her racing heart and allow the adrenalin pumping within her system to ease somewhat. *Well, okay, so that was bad.*

She looked in the pack at the sleeping babies and softly gasped when she saw they were still asleep. *Amazing!*

She re-zipped the bag and knew she could not afford to wait much longer. She was bleeding and the more time she lingered, the weaker she would become then she and the babies would be dead. She felt her shoulder and was relieved to feel the bullet had gone right through, and the blood had slowed courtesy of her shifters fast healing. She grinned knowing her wolf was blocking the pain for her, at times like this she loved being a shifter.

June looked out into the dark forest and chewed on her bottom lip, thinking hard. *How many could be left?* Unfortunately, she was hampered by not knowing how many there had been to start with and they were crafty by not using torches she could not count the ones still alive and mobile.

She was positive she had taken out maybe ten males, but truthfully had lost count, if they were going to use guns, which she knew they would get around to doing again. Regardless of what the loud voiced male said, she needed an advantage.

If she could get to her car, she could stow the babies, then sneak around and take out the others. June thought over her options and decided she liked her plan.

She listened to the fading voices of the males as they moved further away from where she was hiding. When she felt it was safe, she looked out between the bushes and fixed a land mark in her mind, hoping it was close to where she had left her car.

She waited, then checked the babies again they seemed okay. She could feel the blood running inside her clothes from all the sword slices. Knowing she would pay for what she was about to do later if she survived, she asked her wolf to come forth and help her slow the bleeding. Unfortunately, she would not be able to stop the bleeding fully because she was also going to ask her wolf to lend her more strength and energy so she could run faster.

She changed the clips in her guns once more and scented the air there was no one close to her. So she heaved herself up, checked her guns again, and then fixed the target in her sights and with her wolfs energy she took a deep breath and as she exhaled she broke from her hiding place and ran.

She traveled at an angle to the path she had taken on her way up the mountain and had almost made it to her car when she was set upon again. Before she realized what was happening, two males rose from behind bushes as she went to run pass them. It was a race to see who would recover from the surprise her sudden appearance made first.

Twisting left to right, trying to see both assailants in the small clearing, June was slashed with a sword across her back as she was half way into a pivot, throwing her off balance. So much so that the momentum of the sword scraping against her back made her fall into the other male who had come to stand in front of her, his sword raised for his own strike?

She held securely to her guns as she pushed them against his chest and shot repeatedly, he screamed as he fell away from her and was dead when he hit the ground. She stepped sideways just in time to miss the next sword strike from the first male and twisted half a turn and pulled her triggers. Firing repeatedly into his chest and throat, shredding him as he fell backward.

She turned once more breathing heavily as two more males came into the small blood soaked clearing, they stood back away from her. June stood with her guns ready she was still a distance from her car and prayed these were the last two males that were hunting her.

"Give us the abominations and we will let you live." Snarled a tall thin male who stank of alcohol and body odor. His hair hung in long dirty brown braids and his clothes looked like he had slept in them forever and were as dirty as he was.

June scented the air between them, and once she got passed the unwashed smell, she knew they were both human. The shorter of the two was not as dirty as the male next to him. His short black hair was clean, in fact he looked a lot cleaner and only slightly rumpled, compared to the taller male. Unfortunately, the manic look in his eyes behind his glasses bespoke of crazy. June grinned and knew she looked just as crazy as the male, evidenced by the step they both took backward.

"As if assholes. I know damn well you killed these baby's parents and you deserve to die and will." She snarled, anger and pain making her normal voice harsher. "Consider this assholes, if these infants are abominations wait until you see what comes for you next. Now leave. I give you a free pass to say your goodbyes to any foolish enough to love you."

They both laughed at her as they looked her over, from the amount of blood covering her she was obviously wounded with that thought adding to his bravado the tall male snarled. "You think to scare us woman?"

June wheezed out a laugh. "I, by myself, have killed twelve of you. How many do I have to kill to drive home the point that you will never lay a hand on these babies?"

The short male who June thought sounded like a fanatical crazy man snarled. "You are not saving innocents, they carry the gene of the devil within them. They must not be allowed to live."

In answer, June growled deep in her throat, saying. "Exactly how I feel about you, except I have more of a chance of killing you like I did those others you set on me than you have of taking these babies from me. So choose death or to live another day."

She aimed her guns higher and it appeared as though they both realized she may be covered in blood but she was not weakened and was still standing strong. They looked at each other and then the impact of what she had said about killing their fighters seemed to hit them and as one they turned and started to run.

She swapped out a gun for a small blow pipe and quickly blew two small darts hitting both males in their necks, they screamed and slapped at their necks as they felt the hits but did not slow down.

June grinned she had tagged both males for the hunters to find later. Her job was done, she took stock of where she was and saw she was only minutes away from her car, her grin turned into a laugh as she congratulated herself on her plan.

She started the walk to her vehicle. It seemed to take her a lot longer than she thought it should to get to her car. When she did finally make it, she was relieved to see it was still intact and safe. She cancelled the spells and unlocked the doors, then spent several long minutes deciding how to get the straps for the pack undone.

Finally, she pulled her knife and just sliced them in half, she placed the bag with its precious cargo on the front seat and walked around to the trunk, retrieving the med-kit. Sitting on the edge of the trunk, she saw to the wounds she could reach and stopped the blood which had started seeping from her shoulder and arms and legs.

Once she was patched up as well as she could do by herself, she closed the trunk and eased into the driver's seat any energy her wolf had given her was long gone, exhaustion rode her hard. She unzipped her pack and looked inside to see that both babies were still asleep. "If I didn't know better, I would suspect a spell." She bit her lip and mumbled. "Maybe, it is a spell, whatever little ones, stay asleep a little longer. Mama will get us home. We only have to get to a place where I can activate the emergency signal or bat signal as Frankie calls it. Then we will be rescued."

Sadly she had forgotten she did not have her sat phone or any other way to communicate for help, having left all her equipment in the cave.

CHAPTER SIX:

C harlie eyed the male as he walked into her office and barely kept the sigh from escaping. She had no more news today than she did the day before.

"It has been five days, Charlie. Where is she?"

"Fin, I told you yesterday, we are looking for her. The last one to see her was Ella."

"That was two days ago. She could be hurt somewhere, and no one has found her." Fin tried to keep the snarl from his voice, but his dragon was close to the surface as he had been since they realized June had left Dragon's Gap.

Charlie stood and just kept the snarl from her own voice. "That is unfair. We are looking for her. I have retrievers out hunting her now, as I told you yesterday, she never told Ella where she was going. Her phone is down or lost and her GPS is disabled."

"That is not enough."

"I know Fin. We are looking. I swear."

He stared at her for several seconds, then nodded and stormed from her office just before Sage walked in from the connecting door between their offices. "We have scried for her. We cannot find her, was that Fin?"

"Yes, he is angry."

"Aren't we all? Where can she be?"

"I don't know Sage, but I trust her, she is cunning. She will come home."

"She had better." She held her finger and thumb a little apart. "I am that close from calling out the Hunters and Shields."

"Not yet. Give our people time to search."

Sage nodded. "Twenty-four hours."

"Okay Sage, thanks."

She said nothing as she left, but not before giving Charlie the same look she had been giving her every day since June had not returned. Charlie fell into her chair as she looked at the photo of her kids and Storm. "Where are you, June? Please don't get dead."

Fin strode from Charlie's office, he knew she was doing everything she could but he and his dragon could do more. He made his apartment and kept going, reaching his bedroom whereby he started to pull clothes and equipment from his closet. His dragon said. *We leave to find our shadow?*

Yes, we need a few things first.

Then we go.

Yes, to bring her home.

Good, I want shadow.

You and me both. Fin shook his head as he packed a dragon bag full of equipment, first aid packs and blankets, food and water. He knew this was his fault, his stubborn refusal to accept June's needs caused her to be out there alone without his protection.

"Are you going to look for her?" Ella asked tearfully from the doorway to his bedroom. He turned quickly at the sound of her voice he was so concerned for June he had not heard her enter his apartment. "I am."

"I am sorry, Uncle Fin. I should have gone with her or asked where she was going. I just left her."

He dropped his bag and took her trembling body in his arms. "This is not your fault, it is all mine, my belief I could control everything and look what I did. I drove her away."

"She loves you."

"Does she? I do not know how she could."

"Well, when you find her, ask her."

"I will find her niece. I swear."

"I know you will."

"Thank you, now I must go."

"Take care and bring her home."

He smiled, a quick motion of his lips. Ella could see his dragon in his eyes as he assured her. "We will."

He left the castle and entered the grounds where dragons arrived and left from. Ark and Axl were waiting to secure the bag on his back. "I had no idea." Fin stated a little taken aback by the brother's assistance.

"We figured today would be the day you would go, if she had not returned."

"I thank you."

They waited for him to shift, then they strapped the bag on his back. Once they moved away he shook his large body to settle everything. A sixty- five-foot green dragon with purple eyes looked down at the two brothers who called out to him.

"Good hunting."

He bowed his head and lifted gently from the ground, and with one huge flap of his wings, he flew from the castle grounds. Reighn walked from around the corner as he watched the departing dragon. "He has more restraint than I do."

Ark agreed. "Or us."

"Think he will find her?" Axl asked.

Reighn nodded. "It is what he finds that worries me."

They both grimaced at his words, knowing that for Fin to lose June would more than likely turn him rogue. Which would cause Reighn to have to issue an order for his death.

Ark stated. "Well nothing to do now but wait."

"Hate waiting, maybe we should have gone with him?" Axl muttered.

Reighn shook his head. "Fin is deadly, and determined, he will be okay."

It took Fin the rest of the day to track June's movements. He started at the coordinates the driver of the bus gave him, from there he traced June to the car park where her vehicle had been parked. Next he tracked her progress up the side of the mountain. It was very difficult, June was immensely talented at leaving virtually no tell-tale signs of her passage.

Whether it was her innate ability as a wolf or just experience, it was hard to say. All he knew was that June was alive and climbing a mountain, several times he found himself having to back track to pick up her trail. He knew he was on the right path when he found the first of several bullet-ridden bodies.

He tracked her to her hide-away wanting to examine it. He was forced to shift to human, he placed his pack on his back with the simple expediency of shortening the straps to accommodate his smaller human form. Once satisfied, he parted the bushes and crouched down reading the signs she had left behind. He saw where she had rested, and where she had emptied out her guns, stray casings lay scattered on the ground. He moved the leaf matter away and found small puddles of blood. Despair rode his dragon hard.

We know nothing.

His dragon fretted. *She is bleeding.*

I would be surprised if she was not. We need to search more, and we need more information.

His dragon did not offer another comment as Fin sighed, then cocked his head on the side as he saw a clear footprint. The first he had found. Either he was getting better at reading her, or she was panicked and did not care who followed her.

He thought about that for a minute. It did not ring true if she was being hunted she would not leave a trail behind her for hunters to find, and he knew June did not panic.

He stood and looked around, staying in human form, and began tracking her by reading the signs of her passage through the forest He found bullets imbedded in the trunks of several trees. Then he started finding bodies, it seemed as though animals had been picking over the carcasses, but there was enough left to know the males had been shot in some cases repeatedly. He walked farther until he came to a place where he scented June's blood and saw where her hands made impressions in the dirt, looking back along the ground he found her blood not as much as he feared but enough to know she had been hurt. He could feel the anger of his dragon simmering.

I know we will find her. She is hurt, yes, but still alive.

His only answer was a hissing grunt.

His dragon was hunting for his shadow and the ones who had done this, Fin kept moving and found three more bodies. His June had been involved in a sword and gun fight, evidenced by the dead males with swords by their hands and bullets in their bodies. So far he had counted thirteen dead, it appeared his June was a very good shot, despite his fear for her, he was impressed at the carnage she caused.

He looked up from the male's body and saw the mouth of the cave and knew June at one time entered there. Bent over he ran the tunnel coming to the cavern, he saw immediately where she had emptied her bag and as he scented the air, he could smell faint traces of her and something else, something sweeter. It was just barely traceable and was not a scent he had encountered before, he and his dragon were puzzled.

What made June risk her life, and what was it she found that someone wanted to kill her for.

His dragon told him. *All good questions, which we will ask our shadow when we find her. But we will not find her here. Standing looking at stone.*

Fin shook himself and agreed, scooping June's belongings and stuffing them into his bag, he entered the tunnel and turned back; with a breath of flame he destroyed all evidence of her and the sweet scent of the unknown substance in the cave.

When he was outside he slipped the pack on and shifted to dragon, he had a trajectory now. All he needed to do was follow it, and he would have his shadow in his arms once more.

Unfortunately, his tracking had taken more time than he had realised, and he was forced to find a clearing to rest in as night fell along with the rain. Angered at his inability to carry on searching, he curled up in dragon form and waited the night out, fear for his shadow uppermost in his mind, neither he nor his dragon had much to say throughout the night.

Finally, as dawn crept over the sky and the rain ceased, he took to the early morning air and flew back to the car park and started their search from there. His dragon's eyes tracing the signature of the car along dirt roads, many times they had to land

and then backtrack to find the trail. Finally coming to a dirt road that looked like it had suffered severe damage due to the previous night's rain.

They landed, and Fin shifted to human and walked the road, eventually finding where her car had gone off. It looked like she drove down a hill and into a gully, he thought at first she had been pushed off the road but once he shifted back to his dragon and pulled the car from the ravine, he realized she had just lost control.

She was unconscious and wounded he could scent the infections and dried blood and something else, something sweeter. It confused him and his dragon, shifting to human again, he pulled open her door to find June was still in her seat belt and the smell of something foul filled the air of the vehicle.

"June, little wolf, it is Fin. Wake for me my wolf. Wake!" He growled, fear making his voice gruff.

Her eyes remained shut, but he heard her say weakly. "Fin?"

He held her head back and tipped some water between her dry lips and sharply snarled. "Little wolf, wake up!"

June heard him, heard her dragon, and wondered how he had got there, she murmured. "Tired everything foggy... need to rest, just shut my eyes for a minute."

She had pulled over a little off the road, to gather her energy to release the bat signal, needed to rest just for a minute. She was so very tired. Why was Fin here? He had left her, he was gone. Maybe she was dreaming again.

Then a picture of the small babies in her bag flashed across her mind and she huskily muttered. "Babies... babies." As her hands flapped around urgently.

"Hush June, what baby?"

"Bag..." She mumbled, then passed out again.

He saw a black pack on the floor, reaching pass her he pulled it to him and unzipped it. Looking inside he saw two little bodies with pink hair. *Oh shit, we have to go!*

No kidding, where did our shadow get pink haired babies from?

I have no idea. At least we know what that sweet scent is.

43

June roused again, and her hand found his cheek. "Fin… babies… safe… promise."

He kissed her fingers as they curled around his hand and would have promised her the world right then and there. He was so happy she was alive and with him. "I promise little wolf."

But she did not hear, she was unconscious again.

We leave. Now! His dragon demanded. *Strap bag with hatchlings to our shadow and we will take her in my claws.*

Right… Right! Said a slightly befuddled Fin as he hurried to do as his dragon instructed. All his mind wanted to do was dwell in a mixture of relief at finding June alive and awe for the two hatchlings. Were these young ones the reason she had risked her life, what of their parents? He had seen no evidence of them in the cave.

Before he realized it, he was dragon again, and holding June in his large claws. She clutched the bag with the babies, even though he had securely tied it to her chest. Then he flew like he had never flown before to Dragon's Gap and home.

CHAPTER SEVEN:

F in carried June along the corridor to the castle's infirmary. Still unconscious, she nevertheless held the bag with the two small bundles within tightly in her arms.

Fin knew he left a trail of blood from her opened wounds as they walked into the medical unit, while his dragon bellowed for Ella or Sharm.

He was surprised at how fast they arrived, he was not to know just then they had not long finished cleaning up after Harper's arrival and near death. Fin told Ella as she went to take the bag from June. "Pack has babies in it."

With a nod, she gently cut the straps tied around June and immediately lifted the bag off or tried to. Ella softly asked her.

"June release the bag sweetie, so I can check the babies please June."

She would not. Ella was sure her arms held them tighter as she spoke to her. Fin leaned to her. "Little wolf let them go. Ella has them now; we are safe."

Her hands fell away instantly, as soon as the bag was free from her hold. Sharm started assessing her wounds.

Ella laid the bag on the other bed and unzipped it, just as Charlie hurried in, passing Fin as he reached out for the door on his way to get Sage. His hand had only touched the door when they were thrust open by a pale Sage, she took one look at his face and said. "I was on my way to bed when I heard you calling. How is she?"

Fin shook his head. "Alive, be prepared we brought more than June back."

"What?" He motioned to the table that Ella stood at, as she

gently removed and unwrapped babies from the bag.

"Oh my Goddess."

Fin told Sage as he stood hands by his sides, feeling useless and unable to comprehend what he was really seeing. "She made me promise to keep them safe. I believe they are ours, hers and mine. It seems my shadow has made me a daddy."

Charlie came next to him, with her hand in Storms as his arm held her securely to his side. So far the last two days had been hard for his shadow, first her sister and now June. She was feeling quite vulnerable as she asked Fin. "Do you know what happened?"

Fin turned his black eyes on her and Storm's hand twitched, Charlie sighed and laid her hand over his heart. "Hush, he means nothing by it, you can see he is on the edge."

"Stand down, Fin. I understand how you feel but believe me this will not help and June will be the first to tell you so. Also, she can yip, it is very annoying." Reighn said as he entered.

Fin growled and smiled at the same time, it was a weird combination, but he did know the yipping could drive a dragon to drink. Charlie asked. "How did you find her?"

"Tracked her from the point when she entered the portal through our connection, it is very thin, very faint. It only got me so far, the rest was luck and knowledge and hard won experience. Once I found where the portal opened up for her, it was just a case of following the signs, so I had to get real close."

They all knew there was far more to it than he was saying, but it was not the time now to examine everything he had done to find his shadow. He told them quietly. "Her car was off the road, she had gone down a hillside landed in a ravine covered in bush easily missed."

Charlie's lips tightened as she looked at Sage and said. "We need to teach our people tracking; they rely too much on the Hunters."

Fin heaved in a deep breath and held it as his eyes became wild and he started to shake, letting go of the breath, he suddenly realized how close he had come to loosing June. Storm grabbed his shoulder. "I know old friend, I know. She will be alright, Sharm, and your Ella will make it so."

Fin nodded and Frankie slipped under his arm as Sage did the same on the other side. "Come on, Fin; we are here for you." Frankie told the huge male.

"Family." Sage softly said. "We stick together, she will be alright she's a fighter. You know she is. We all know that."

Hoarsely, he said. "I know... I know."

Ella called to Sage. "Sage, I think the babies are under a sleep spell; they will not wake, and I am sure they will need food. We need Edee as well."

Sage gave Fin's arm a pat in comfort as she moved to Ella just as Edith arrived. "I am here. Oh my, pink hair."

"That is all you can say?" Sage asked as she turned to where Edith came to a stop. "Well what else. I mean pink."

"I don't know, something like where did they come from? What species are they, anything other than just pink?"

Edith hummed, then said. "So cute. Molly will be jealous." Sage grinned, knowing it will not be Molly as much as it would be Cara who will be jealous.

It was a well-known fact, Cara thought as a unicorn she should have pink hair. Why she thought this, no one knew. It was what she asked for almost daily, to the point Storm asked Sage to change the color of her hair? She had declined, especially when Charlie gave her a long look of retribution if she had dared too. Sage hid a laugh she knew Charlie was going to have a fight on her hands, because she was always telling Cara nobody had pink or purple hair other than faeries. She looked over at the worried Charlie and saw she had not realized that yet.

Placing her hands over both of the baby's eyes and foreheads, saying a few words while a soft blue mist engulfed her hands and flowed out to enfold each little body in a blue light, then the light winked out. Within seconds the babies opened their eyes and started to cry softly as new-borns did.

"Green eyes, now that is even cuter." Edith murmured as she placed a hand over each little chest. "Pixie and faerie. Wow, I did not think that was a thing?"

"Not usually." Reighn agreed as he moved to where the young were. "Although Elijah is pixie."

Edith grinned. "Yeah, I forget that. So they are two days old or one day. Fin pick one because of the spell it can be either."

"One day." He said unsure why that felt right, but it was what he decided, so he stuck with it.

She nodded. "One day it is." Mentally, she recorded the date. Ella and Sage changed both babies into clean clothes while a bottle for each was warmed. Sage grinned at Reighn as she told him. "Well... well look at that, I am an auntie and you are an uncle again."

Charlie just stared and slowly lifted her eyes to Fin's stunned one's saying. "This is not going to end well."

Fin replied quietly. "I know, they will never let us keep them?"

Reighn rubbed his head as he stared at the babies. "How the hell did our June get them?"

"Does it matter, they are June's and Fin's?" Frankie asked of him.

Reighn looked at her and frowned. "Unfortunately, nothing is that simple." He asked Fin. "Do you want them?"

"My shadow was bringing them home, this means something. So until she says they are not ours. I will keep them."

Sharm straightened and stretched his back, then walked to where they all stood. "So it is a good news... bad news scenario."

"Good news first please, my friend." Fin said as Sage braced herself.

"I have healed all her wounds, sword and bullet holes. Someone tried real hard to kill our June."

Sage sucked in a breath through her teeth, then said as Fin's face hardened even more. "Just as well, she is hard to kill."

"Isn't it, though?" Agreed a sardonic Sharm. "Bad news, she was poisoned, with a type of human poison, it was designed to drain the life force of a half-shifter. A human or someone who knows magic has developed this."

"Is it fairy magic?" Fin asked, shocked that faeries would kill one of their own.

"Sort of and yet no, it is magic with a twist and it is the twist I have no cure for."

"Sharm my brother, that is as clear as dirt." Sage grumbled.

"I know." He wiped his face. "So plainly, the poison is draining her life-force, thankfully she is wolf and has the shifters ability to heal just about anything; this is helping to slow it down. But it will win if we do not find help, I took samples and may be able to manufacture an antidote but do not hold your breath. Dragon Lady, someone is misusing magic. Your department, I think?"

Sage snarled. "It is and someone will pay."

"This may help, it is a variation of what felled Storm."

With a look at his shadow's strained face and Fin's closed one. Reighn said. "I am tired of this. It seems like every time we turn around, we are confronted with another type of poison. Call the Faeries."

Charlie nodded as she pulled her phone out as Sharm turned toward the two babies. "Now, who do we have here, it appears as though we have two little faeries."

Ella nodded in agreement as Edith smiled saying. "Half right. Pixie and faerie, what a combination. Their parents were brave, very brave to go against the faerie rules must have been love."

Fin took his eyes from the green eyed, pink haired babies and looked at the erected screens where his June was being washed. He looked at Reighn and asked. "What do I do?"

"Well, my friend." Reighn shook his head as he told him. "Your shadow has brought you trouble. June has taken them as yours, which means before she wakes, we have some decisions to make."

"First thing." Sage said. "Let us get the faeries here. Who is available?"

Charlie grimaced. "Only Prince Tarin again."

"Why, Scarlett and Elijah were here earlier with Kai."

Charlie nodded. "True, but they all returned to the High Queens Grove before the confinement starts.

Sage pouted. "Shoot."

This announcement was met with silence until Sage shrugged and said. "Call him anyway; we will do damage control later."

Charlie nodded. "I have already."

Sage told them. "Look, let's see what we are dealing with here, it may not be as bad as we think."

CHAPTER EIGHT:

Fifteen minutes later, Sage's hopes were dashed. "They have to go to the Grove." The Prince announced pompously, putting everyone's teeth on edge.

"Do their lives depend on it?" Fin asked mildly as he watched Verity coo to his daughters in their baskets.

"No, not their lives but..."

"But nothing," he answered, "they stay until their mother says otherwise."

Reighn grunted and hid a smile. Tarin had been at the Grove for almost five months visiting the Queen and King. In that time he had been allowed the run of Dragon's Gap. He had heard, if it had not been for his personal guards, he would surely be dead. It was unfortunate Elijah and Scarlett were absent. When Tarin had arrived, and Reighn had asked him to look the hatchlings over. He had taken one look and started making pronouncements and demands.

First, he demanded to know how June had obtained the twins, which they had no answer for.

Sage had told him it appeared June had rescued two half-blood faeries only a day old, and until she woke, they were still in the dark. Sharm had explained that somewhere between dropping her car load of females and their young off, and Fin finding her. She apparently encountered people with swords and guns that tried to kill her.

The Prince nodded several times when Sharm and Sage finished recounting the events leading up to him being summoned. Then he decided he had not pissed Fin off enough, he smirked as he said. "Dragon Fin, I do not think you realize the political dilemmas you will be causing by not giving the half-breeds to me."

Reighn wondered if the male could get anymore patronizing. Fin replied. "You are right, but that makes no difference to what will happen. Especially if you want to remain alive."

Reighn watched Tarin try to bend Fin to his will. He had reports of the male having the occasional temper tantrum that faeries were known for and he had of course had the run in with Ace over Joy. But as he had stayed away from her, and Axl had only threatened to kill him once. All seemed to be settling down. His own guards had made sure he was never in Dragon's Gap at the same time as Joy. The hurt feelings he had caused in the first two months after his arrival had been easily settled by either Frankie or June.

Getting nowhere with Fin Tarin tried another tactic and decided better option would be to demand, not persuade or convince. No, just demand that the hatchlings be removed from the castle, preferably Reighn was sure before June woke and decided to use her guns.

He could see Sage was furious, her friend and sister, lay unable to defend herself or her hatchlings, and this male thought to take them from her. This was not going to end well for the Prince, because Reighn knew just like he knew the sun would come up tomorrow, that his shadow would never allow those hatchlings to be taken.

That was, of course, if Fin even thought to allow it, this was not going to happen regardless of what the prince said. There was no one more stubborn than his friend Finlay Slorah, who had said only a handful of words since the male arrived, which consisted mainly of no.

Tarin was getting annoyed, his guards who understood and read the anger in the room better than the Prince, were becoming restless. If the clenching and unclenching of their sword hands were any indication. Any minute now the prince was going to screw up, and Reighn was going to let him. He did not like the male and had very little patience for him. With the next words out of the male's mouth, Reign was proved right.

"I do not think you understand dragon Slorah. These half-breeds belong at the Grove, but under the circumstances it will have to be the Northern Grove, where I will undertake their re-education, it is what must happen. You and your female are not permitted to keep what you do not own. That is if they survive the next few days, which I doubt, as half- breeds do not survive when they are early birthed. Regardless, we own the half-breeds as is our right. So I demand you hand them over to me now." As the prince spoke, his voice had risen enough for all to hear.

Fin straightened from his relaxed pose against the door frame leading into the utility room. The twins had been fed, bathed and changed and were now resting in baskets Verity and Grace had found for them. They looked adorable, every now and again his eyes drifted to them and his dragon crooned in pleasure. All he wanted to do was take his family to the home waiting for them. So his brogue was more pronounced with the impatience he felt and his dragon's anger at the delays as he said. "I understand you are a prince and that you have only been here a short while. I have been here less, even though it is my home. So I am going to let your poor choice of words pass. Other than to say Dragon's Gap, has no half-breeds, which includes these hatchlings here. So if I was you, I would rephrase what you are trying to say and before you speak again. Think. Now as to the matter of removing my hatchlings to a Grove, any Grove. It will not happen."

Just then four small figures flew into the room as they landed they grew and Fin raised an eyebrow in amusement. Prince Tarin swirled around and bowed as Queen Scarlett and King Elijah with their guards appeared.

Displeasure radiated from the Queen and King, the Prince again unable or unwilling to read the feelings emanating from the new arrivals and thinking he now had substantial backing. As well as ignoring the warning looks his guards threw him, puffed out his chest and said. "Oh please, dragon Slorah, you were say-ing?"

Fin eyed the male and his guards and then the newcomers,

shrugged and said as he straightened from the wall where he had relaxed back too. "I was going to say, I have no idea what re-education is, nor do I care to know. What I do know is that my shadow, not my female as you so eloquently put it, will not allow her babies to be taken by you or anyone. I, of course, will have to agree with her. They are our hatchlings, not yours, they stay here with us."

Tarin inclined his head in a mocking salute to Fin. "I understand what you are saying, we of course must take into consideration the feelings of your shadow, maybe we could come to some arrangement."

Reighn stood, head bowed as Sage looked over at him uncomprehendingly when she heard him mumble. "Do not say it you fool, it is not worth your life."

Tarin smirked as he said. "We could, of course, offer a monetary compensation for the half... Sorry young."

Every female growled at his audacity as anger swamped Sage and she threw a blue ball of magic at the male, dropping him to his knees. "You dare! My sister's hatchlings are not property to be bought and sold. You disrespect our young and disrespect our home."

She lifted her eyes to the screen June was meant to be lying behind and found her standing there,, her eyes were on fire as they locked on Fin, he was by her side in a second. "No, my love... No, they will remain with us. I will never allow it. Your family will not allow it. Come, let me take you back to bed." She nodded and looked at Sage, who said. "I have this, go my sister."

June sighed and her eyes rolled back up into her head as she passed out once more, Fin swept her up into his arms, carrying her back to bed. Claire hurriedly went with them.

Reighn looked at the male now on his knees. "Queen Scarlett, King Elijah, you should explain the facts to the young prince and while you are at it, tell him whose territories these are. It may stop any complications in the future and possibly keep him alive."

They both inclined their heads as the Queen answered. "Thank you for your understanding. The facts will once again be discussed with him."

Sage released him, and he stood scowling at her. The King looked at Reighn. "She will not heal completely without our help. It is why we are here. May we?"

As the Queen eyed the prince, she said. "One of the reasons. You, Tarin, will stay here until we have seen to our friend."

The prince paled when the Queen motioned to the four guards. "Make sure he stays."

Then she said to the two guards that were with the prince. "Daru, Mercca. I apologize once more for your discomfort."

They both bowed, and the one named Daru responded. "It has been illuminating our Queen."

"I am sure it has been." Was the King's dry response as he and his Queen followed Frankie behind the screens.

Reighn turned to the prince. "You are an idiot, aren't you? Is that why you are here?"

"I do not know what you mean. I do not have to answer to you, Dragon Lord." Even now he sneered at Reighn, who took one step toward him only to stop, as Storm was suddenly in front of the male which may have saved his life. He punched him hard in the stomach and dropped him to the floor, looking down at him without expression. Storm was Commander of the Shields and one of the most fearsome of dragons, the prince made to get up, Storm pointed a finger at him as he said.

"Stay down, you fool. You just insulted our Lord, in his home, on his lands. You know you are a guest at his benevolence. You will apologize now." Storm's voice was calm and controlled, which made it all the more frightening.

Tarin gulped the hot words on his tongue while anger with a healthy dose of fear entered his eyes, sulkily he said. "I apologize for my words, Dragon Lord."

Reighn felt his dragon stir at the look of contempt that entered the faerie's eyes. His guards must have felt it as well, because one of them, the one named Mercca decided it was time to introduce himself and Reighn, did wonder if it was to save the prince from

Storm's wrath.

"My Lord, please let me introduce you to our Kings guards, Rumoh and Dumoh. They are brothers and have been with the Queen and King for many years."

They both bowed from the waist and ignored the now trembling prince as he rose. Tarin finally realized the predicament he was in, when none of the royal guards had stopped the male Storm from hitting him or reprimanded him. In fact, they seemed to radiate quiet satisfaction.

"I am Mercca and this is my partner and friend Daru." They also bowed to Reighn and Sage. The guard Daru said. "To answer your previous question. Yes, he is an idiot and yes, that is indeed why he is here. It is his last chance, and he has succeeded in making sure it would fail, to what outcome my friends and I have no idea."

The other guard Mercca told them. "I would also like to apologize for not thumping him in the mouth as I should have or let my partner do it when he was talking earlier. I did not, because Fin was handling it, if I had known June was here. I would not have been so tolerant."

The guard Daru said. "We count both Fin and June among our friends and have spent many delightful days with Fin at Broadswords.

"How dare you?" Tarin spluttered.

Without even looking at the prince, Daru said. "Shut up Tarin, you are beyond your home borders and in trouble. Our Queen is very tolerant, yet even she has had enough. Your parent's last resort was to send you here. So I advise you to be quiet."

The Queen and King re-entered, the Queen enfolded Sage in a hug and said. "She will be well. Elijah rid her of the remaining infection and poison. It was, as Sharm said, a mix of human and faerie magic. We will send the information to the High Queen, and my people will track down how these thugs got a hold of it. We will need to talk to June when she is well. For now, know she will recover and her daughters will thrive and be well enough to give her shadow a merry dance."

Sage laughed and hugged her back. "Thank you, Scarlett. I was worried."

The King hugged her as well. "You are welcomed, she is dear to us, without June, we all would be lost. She is our glue."

"She really is." Sage agreed tearfully.

Elijah said. "Now the young are, as you know, half faerie and half pixie. In as much as I dislike our Queen mother's nephew's words, he is correct in that they will have needs that June and Fin will be unable to manage."

Fin walked out from behind the screen. Elijah nodded to him and continued. "Tarin was incorrect as to where they could receive an education, they will be helped and given their normal tuition here. I am a full-blood Pixie. I am sure Tarin just forgot that or he would have told you I am quite capable of undertaking their education." He held his hand up when Fin went to speak. "It will commence if and only if they show abilities. They are what used to be referred to as gray ones, so abilities can appear at any time."

Charlie said. "So, they do not have to leave our home?"

He smiled. "No niece, they remain with their parents and grace knows they are so very fortunate to have found such wonderful parents and family as sad as it must be, for surely they have lost their birth parents. Fortune shined on them when June answered their call."

Fin said. "June has told me they and their mother sung for her to come to them. She was there with the mother when she passed into the night."

Elijah sighed. "That is the way of some of us. She would have been pixie, we are forever concerned with whom to leave our young too if we are unable to survive. She would have sung and the young would have joined her to call June to them. Do you happen to know her name?"

Fin said quietly. "I do not, June may. I will ask when she is well."

"Thank you Fin."

Sage asked. "What would have happened if June had not been out there to hear their song, would they have reached her here?"

Elijah sighed as he told her sadly. "Maybe, maybe not. Depends how weak the mother was and I think you know what would have happened to the young, dear Sage."

"Oh, it is too terrible to think about." Her hand went to her stomach where her hatchlings rested out the corner of her eye she saw Edith do the same action and sniffed back her smile.

The Queen nodded. "But that did not happen so this is a good time to rejoice for Fin and June and their new daughters. So my Light, what to do with that?" She indicated Tarin with a nod of her head.

A haughty look came over the prince's face as he went to speak. Elijah looked at the male with disgust and flicked his fingers, the prince's mouth snapped closed.

"I have a suggestion." Charlie said as she moved from her Lords side to stand in front of the prince. Storm stood with Reighn who was joined by Johner as Frankie was still with June. "First though uncle, could you release his tongue?"

"Of course."

To the prince, she said. "I know you know who I am and who my sister is?"

He nodded slowly as Charlie stared at the male faerie and her eyes became distant and ghost hard. "Oh, I see you know who we are, good. We are the lost ones, which you know of as the gray ones, and all the rumors you have heard about our kind are quite true. So hear and believe me when I tell you this, because I will only say it once. Now that female in there is our friend and as of now her children are our family and they are off limits to you and any more like you. If anything happens to my nieces or if they mysteriously go missing one night or day a week from now, a month. A year or ever. My sister and I will bring a reign of terror down on you and your kind, the likes of which you have never seen before. And if by some miracle you or your kind take us both out, then her shadow and mine and our combined families in case you missed that. The Queen and King and their Grove, and the Hunters, the Shields, the retrievers. Oh hell, the whole of Dragon's Gap will just finish what we started. **Do I Make Myself Clear?**"

"Yes, you do." The shaken faerie said.

Charlie said to the Queen who had a very blood thirsty look in her eye along with a hint of laughter. "So here is my idea."

Scarlett said. "Yes dear."

"Send this one, without guards to the castle tomorrow. I think he needs an attitude adjustment."

"How does one go about doing that?"

"Frankie?"

"Yes Charlie." Frankie answered as she came from behind the screen, with a pleased look in her eyes.

"You can have him for the first week then if Sharm and Edith do not mind they can have him for the…"

"May I make a suggestion?" Reighn interrupted as he too eyed the hapless male.

"Why yes, dear Lord, you may." Charlie inclined her head.

Reighn sighed, much like his father did on occasion.

"Smart ass, how about sending him to the ones he thinks are no more than breeders and half-breeds."

"Oh, good idea. Yeah, to the healers he can work on the wards and then to the retrievers unit, then the Hunters. Then he can serve in the construction unit for a while."

"Building with his hands may be good for him." Rene ` agreed as he and Verity arrived back from making sure everything was ready for Fin to take June and the babies to her home. Reighn nodded. "Can you manage that, Frankie?"

"I can write a schedule."

Reighn smiled. "Then forward it to me for final approval." He turned to the two royals. "What say you Elijah, Scarlett?"

Tarin outraged at the proposed plan spoke for the first time since Charlie had confronted him. "No, I protest, you have no right to enforce your obscene punishments on me. I have said and done nothing to warrant such a…"

"Be quiet!" A male voice whipped across his senses and filled the room as two more faeries walked in.

"Mother, Father." Tarin dropped his head into his hands. "Thank your graces; you have arrived. I was to be enslaved." He sobbed into his hands.

The male snarled. "Foolish child, stop this embarrassing display of weakness." He said to the female. "He takes after his Uncle Fregan."

"Oh, I know. It is a shame. I do not know where we went wrong with him."

The male sighed. "It is the problem with the youngest. I suspect we were far too soft on him."

"This could be true."

Queen Scarlett bowed her head slightly when she saw the newcomers, smiling she made the introductions. "Dragon Lord Reighn and Dragon Lady Sage, may I introduce you to Queen Isla Ravenswood and King Gideon Ravenswood, the High Queens sister and brother by marriage. Isla, Gideon the Dragon Lord Reighn Kingsley and his shadow Lady Sage Kingsley."

They all bowed their heads. Scarlett then said. "Allow me also to introduce Lord Rene ` and Lady Verity Kingsley, former Lord and Lady of the castle. Then there is our niece Lady Charlie and her shadow Storm Kingsley." She went on introducing everyone else, finally she said. "Isla. I did not know you were coming?"

"Really, and yet we told our son we were."

They all looked at the sulky male. Tarin looked down as he mumbled. "I forgot to tell you."

"Convenient." His father stated. "Well my Light, what should we do with this one. I am out of patience."

"I sympathize with you my dear." She turned her hard gaze on the prince. "Tarin we have been informed you are causing problems. You even attacked a young shifter, ward of Queen Scarlett's niece and her shadow. Is that so?"

He said. "I was misunderstood."

Scarlett growled. "Really, you were caught by her father?"

He protested. "He wasn't then."

"Fool!" His father snarled. "He should have ended you. I would have, if you had done so with my child or Light. Where did you get this idea you are entitled?"

When Tarin opened his mouth, he held his hand up. "I do not want to hear it again."

His mother said. "A generous solution has been broached, so

you can make amends and you have objections?"

Feeling his mother was softening, he whined. "I do mother, they will turn me into a slave."

Reighn said. "That is not so, you will always be allowed to leave my territories. Which is exactly what will happen, if you do not decide to comply?"

His father smiled, a gleam in his eyes. "Tell me, son. Where will you go?"

Once again ignoring his father, he said. "Mother, I will go home." She was shaking her head before he stopped speaking. "No my son, you will not. I asked Meadow, your aunt, for this placement against your father's objections. I felt the dragons and Elijah would be a good influence on you. I find you have squandered the opportunity to become more than a spoiled child."

His father stood in front of Tarin's mother, so he had no option but to look up at his father. "You may not return to our Grove, in fact our High Queen has stated because of your outrageous conduct here all Groves will be closed to you."

Tarin's face paled with horror as he asked. "You would dare to allow this to happen. You could not intervene on my behalf. Am I not your son?"

His father raised one eyebrow at his son as he told him. "We insisted, your mother and I, that your aunt did so."

Outraged, he yelled at his father. "You have no right. I am not a delinquent. I am a Prince!"

"Ooh! He really does need an attitude adjustment." His mother snapped, and with a flick of her fingers he disappeared. "I have sent him to the Groves isolation room."

Amused, Scarlett asked Elijah. "Did you know we have one of those?"

Elijah answered with a decided twinkle in his eyes. "No my Light, I had no idea." He asked Queen Isla. "We have one of those?"

"You do now." King Gideon said with a smile.

Just then two tiny cries were heard from within the baskets. Fin stepped over to where his daughters lay. He reached inside and lifted one tiny bundle out and handed her to Scarlett, who along with Isla had edged nearer to see the babies. Within seconds he had handed the other baby to Queen Isla who cooed at her then said "Oh my Light look at her, are they not both delightful?"

And they were, with their tiny scrunched up faces topped by pink hair, and when they blinked, bright green eyes stared out. Scarlett fell in love. "Absolutely delightful."

Elijah said. "You and June are truly blessed, Fin."

Fin grinned. "In more ways than one."

"So, a little more than faeries when born?" King Gideon stated.

Elijah nodded. "Much more."

"The High Queen will be happy. Pixies are back on Earth." Isla said.

"Hold on, Elijah, you are Pixie? I do not understand you just said they were not on Earth." Asked a confused Sage.

Elijah grinned as he told her. "I come from a very progressive fraction of pixie. My parents, the Luminary. Which is what we call our monarchs, are very future orientated?"

Reighn and Fin gave each other a look, realizing Elijah did not actually answer Sage's question.

Charlie asked. "What are a group of pixies called?"

"Luminaries and we live in a Luminia, similar to a Grove. My parents have no problems about mixing races, thankfully, or I would not have been allowed to join with my Light. Many Luminaries feel the same." He smiled at Scarlett, who smiled back at him.

King Gideon said. "That could be because often as not pixies always breed true."

Elijah grinned. "That could be true but not always accurate."

"And yet by the look of these two, it would seem. I am right."

Elijah inclined his head. "I concede you could be right, although I would guess their mother was of high society."

"Is that why you wanted to know their mothers name?" Fin asked.

"Yes, if I knew her name, we would possibly know what other Luminaries are on Earth and where she came from. Then we could talk to them, they will know she has passed, but they still should be told."

"Will they want her young back?" Frankie asked.

"As to that, I cannot say. Our Luminaries would let the calling stand. What they will do is unknown."

"A moot point until we know who she was." Edith said.

Reighn told them. "I agree, and I would not worry too much. The Elementals will impress on all Luminaries to register with us. At some point they will contact us and tell us when, where and how many are here."

Surprised, Scarlett asked. "Oh, did our High Queen do this?"

Reighn smiled. "She did, which is how we were lucky enough to receive a Grove."

Scarlett smiled back. "It was really our luck."

"Shall we agree to say we both lucked out?" Reighn asked.

"I do not understand. I thought you told Charlie and I, that it was against the rules for faeries to search and bond outside of faeriedom?" Storm asked Elijah.

Elijah and Scarlett both nodded as she replied. "That is still true, although what I should have said was. A Council and former High Queen, probably in the beginning of time, decided that faeries and pixie were of the same tree."

"Oh, so the same family just different branches like cousins, and do pixies feel the same?" Frankie asked Elijah, who smiled as he said. "We do not, but we do not care for purity like the Faerie council did."

Frankie snorted, then said. "That makes sense, but I think the faerie council was splitting hairs."

"As does our new High Queen and King." Queen Isla told them. "Which is why my sister and her Light are working to change the old ways. It will, of course, go much quicker now after what has happened with Harper and the council."

The babies again cried, which put paid to anymore conversation. Verity had everyone leave so she could give Fin his first lesson in changing diapers and feeding hatchlings.

CHAPTER NINE:

June came aware slowly. She was in a strange bed, in a strange room. Her first thought was to run, her second, was not to move, remembering the pain she had experienced. Her third; was where were her babies?

"Babies!" She croaked out.

Fin walked into her line of sight and told her. "You are in our bed, in our house, and our hatchlings are not more than three feet away to your right."

She turned her head and sure enough there were two bassinets standing side by side. She looked back at him, took in the haggard face, the tired eyes and saw his slumped shoulders. He was untidy, as though he had slept in his clothes. June wished she was any-where but here, and whispered.

"Pixies and faeries."

"I know, my June you were poisoned which is why you feel like a steam roller ran you over. I do not know what that is, but Frankie assured me it was what you will feel like."

She tried laughing and wheezed instead. "Oww, sore."

"I know. I am going to lift you, so you can sit, and then I am going to give you a drink of juice, then water. Sharm's orders."

"Okay."

He helped her sit and passed her a tall glass of juice. She drank half of it, then said. "There is a piece of paper in my pack; it has all their information on it."

Fin said as she started drinking the rest of the juice. "I will give it to Elijah. He says he needs to find out where their birth parents came from."

"Okay, I sort of promised we would keep them." She told him as she reached for the glass of cold water.

Fin smiled. "We will keep them."

It was weird the more she drank the thirstier she became, she finished the next glass of water he handed her, finally feeling her thirst quench. Then looked him in the eyes. "You do not have to feel obliged, I did not promise for you."

Taken a little aback, Fin tried to keep the growl from his voice. "June, I know I have been an ass. In fact I have been more than that, but I have lived in fear that I would fail you, fail any young we could have."

June's eyes remained shuttered as she asked. "What has changed?"

Fin rubbed his hands over his tired eyes and face. "Truthfully, everything, you left me, and I realized I cannot prepare for everything. I thought I needed to make sure you would be safe. I thought I needed to know that no one or nothing could take you from me." He sighed as he held his face in his hands, then lifted shattered eyes to hers. "You know what happened to Ella's parents. I decided I would never ever allow that to happen to you or our young."

June wanted to hug him, wanted to take that look from his eyes, instead she asked softly, "And now what do you think?"

"That I was a fool, I can prevent and prepare for most things, but I did not take into account you. My little wolf... My June. I cannot safe guard against you leaving me." He hung his head and June's face softened as he whispered. "I swear June. I cannot live these last five days again. Where I did not know if you were alive or dead. I missed you so much, and my dragon pined so much I thought he would die. That is when I realized that was what your wolf was doing. Pining for me, for our lives to start and I am so very sorry."

She placed her hand on his cheek. He took it and kissed her fingers as they curled around his hand, his eyes remorseful, she glimpsed his sad and fearful dragon looking out at her.

"If I wasn't feeling like a pancake, I would show you how much you mean to me. I am so sorry that you had to go through that."

Fin kissed her hands and her lips, finally resting his head on her shoulder as he told her tiredly. "Sometimes males like me need to be hit with a four by two or so Edee says, to realize what they have to lose."

June grinned, her poor Fin had been hauled over the coals by her family. "Someone hit you?" She asked, a little outraged and slightly amused that someone had attacked her Fin.

He shrugged. "It could have been worse, it could have been Sage or Edee."

At that, June laughed as she asked. "So where is everyone?"

"They were all here, but Verity and Grace chased them all away. Do not leave me my love, we, my dragon, and I will not survive."

"I promise my heart. I will not, my wolf and I found out we love you too much to leave you."

"You love me?"

"Of course, you and your dragon are ours."

"Why... Why, would you love me, after what I have done?"

"Oh my love. I can honestly say you make me feel like a whole person, someone of worth. I believed my whole life I would never find anyone like you and yet here you are, all mine. You are my shield or will be once you commit to me."

"I have committed, we are your shield against everyone and everything. You will always be mine forever."

June brushed his chin with her finger and kissed him softly. "Yep, yours forever. Sleep now."

As he laid down beside her, she rubbed his chest until he fell asleep. June dozed beside him for a little while until sometime later Sage opened the door and looked round the edge of it. Seeing she was awake, she smiled and drew closer, whispering. "Want to get up?"

"You have no idea. I need to use the bathroom and shower so bad." She whispered back with a grin, still pale, but her strength was returning, making her feel better.

Sage grinned in return. "Okay, I will help you out."

Together they wiggled her out from under Fin, who had managed to lay over half of her. Once she was standing, she looked down on the huge male. "I don't think anything will wake him."

Sage agreed saying. "It has been days since he slept."

June groaned. "Way to make me feel even guiltier."

Sage looked at her with rounded eyes as she said. "Oh, sorry, really didn't mean too!"

"Such a bad liar." June sniffed in disbelief as Sage shrugged. "Well okay, you sort of deserve it, you know?"

"I know."

"Well, it is justified, you gave us a fright. I worried, and that means Reighn worried and then he roared at Fin. Which made Fin roar, which was not pleasant, just so you know."

June scowled at her. "Got it."

"I was just saying."

"Sage, is there a reason you want to make me roar?"

Sage watched her cover Fin gently with a blanket as June's eyes lifted to hers. She raised her eyebrows. "No, not really, just wanted to make my point."

"Consider it made sister." June growled. Then before she could snap at Sage again, she grabbed her in a hug hard enough to crack a rib and whispered. "Wolf crazy, seriously June, I thought you had got pass all that?"

June returned the hug, although gentler. "Me too, I think what I considered rejection, made me revert to that time in my life when I was just crazy. I am very sorry, I swear it will not happen again. I have you, our family and Fin as well as the girls now. My wolf and I realize that we have more to lose maybe it took this lesson for my wolf and I to understand."

"Maybe." Sage agreed, she honestly hoped so.

They looked into the bassinets at the two pink haired babies. "Like cotton candy." Sage murmured.

June smiled. "I know, we could call one cotton and the other one candy?"

"No, Elijah wanted me to ask if you knew who their mother and father were."

"Oh yeah, I told Fin, but..." They looked at the comatose male who snored softly and smiled, June gave her the same information she had given Fin.

Sage grinned. "Thanks hon' now go take your shower. See that little alcove there?" She pointed to a small room that looked like it could be used for a small sitting room. "We have set up a nursery in there, changing table, cupboards with clothes, etc., until they are older. I knew you would not want them away from you, there is a baby monitor as well. So shower come down to the kitchen, we will hear them when they wake."

"Thank you Sage, for everything" She indicated the baby room knowing it was her idea.

Sage shrugged as she said. "Who loves yah baby?"

June chortled as she walked toward her bathroom. "You do, you big sucker." Then laughed as she closed the bathroom door behind her.

Sage watched her go, then when the door closed she took a breath and let the tears fall as she pushed each bassinet into the newly made baby room. June was alright, she and Fin would bond. All they had to do was find out who wanted the babies and if they had a right to them. Olinda and Keeper were pouring over all the information they could find about Pixie Law.

Elijah was helping as much as he could unfortunately, each Luminia was autonomous. So what he knew about his Luminia may not apply to the girls birth mothers.

She had not told June or Fin that they already had a demand for the babies to be returned to their birth fathers Grove. Sage feared they may not be able to stop the Pixie Luminary from taking them either.

She slipped the paper from the pack into her pocket she would give this to Reighn and Elijah and hope she was wrong. She had a bad feeling about all this

.

CHAPTER TEN:

Deciding to meet June in the kitchen, Sage closed the door from the bedroom and walked down the wide staircase of June's home.

Her hand glided over the chunky polished wood of the banister as the stairs curved down to the foyer. It was one of the most beautiful and large entryways Sage had ever seen in a home; the castle did not count.

She hurried to the foyer table and placed the paper inside the waiting envelope, sealed it and then whispered a few words and the envelope vanished Reighn would receive it immediately. She loved being a witch.

She stared at the full-length stained glass panels beside the huge wooden front doors, which a dragon could enter through. The colored glass had a design of a dragon on each panel, it was well done and unless studied would be missed; she wondered if June knew they were dragons.

The home had hardwood floors throughout which would be good for crawling girls, although she thought maybe the priceless rose patterned rug in the entryway may have to go. Which was a shame, it was beautiful. Maybe June could put it in her home office.

Rene` had told June when he gifted the house and fifty acres to her, his mother had always dreamed of a cabin in the woods. This five bedroom log home was the closest his father could come to a cabin, for a dragon it was considered small and a cabin.

Rene` had said his mother had loved it. Probably because his father had built it for her, even though it was a far cry from her simple little cabin she had talked of.

Sadly, after his parent's death, he and Andre` had allowed the home to fall into disrepair, partly through youth and partly he admitted because it was painful for them. Memories of their parents haunted the home, they very seldom visited the cabin, even now.

When June had arrived at Dragon's Gap, Reighn had asked his father and uncle ` if they would allow it to be gifted to her. They had immediately agreed, thankful someone would live in it and love the house again, in all honesty they were thankful the weight of not looking after it, was removed from their hearts.

Sage remembered the day Reighn brought her and June to the house, it was run down; the yard surrounding it was an overgrown bush land and there was no driveway like there was now, or wrought-iron gates. The place was an unloved wasteland of broken dreams. Panes of glass had been broken or just removed from the windows and the wooden logs that the house was made from were lack-lustre, due to the weather beating on them. The roof needed repair and the stone fireplace was missing stones and yet with one look at the large log cabin. June had fallen in love.

Since then, under her tender loving care, the home had a complete renovation. The outside had lawns and gardens; she had a driveway added as well as walls and gates. The roof was renewed, and the logs refurbished. Inside saw updated plumbing and electricity as well as modern bathrooms added and the wooden floors and walls all refinished. The stone fireplace in the great hall or lounge was renewed and the missing stones found and replaced. The room had cathedral style ceilings with old-fashioned chandeliers, which were cleaned and electric lighting installed the floors were re-polished, and the fireplace and chimney were cleaned. Curtains and rugs were added throughout to make the house a cozy home.

Sage was positive the country kitchen was what June had fallen in love with and had sealed the deal, everyone knew she loved to cook and bake. Once Rene` became aware of that, he made sure the kitchen was upgraded for a chef with a six burner stove and large appliances. Granite counters, and wooden cupboards with a butler's pantry were also added.

A large kitchen table sat before the sun drenched glass doors leading out to an outside patio which led down and around to a swimming pool and tennis court. There were stables out back that lay empty now, although Sage had heard June allowed unicorns to graze here.

She had no idea June had been furnishing her home, but everywhere she looked she could see June's fingerprints all over the house all done with love and care. She just knew Rene ` and Andre ` would love how she had restored the home and be pleased at the love and attention she had showered on the home their father had built for their mother.

CHAPTER ELEVEN:

S age entered the kitchen and was met with a divine aroma, Grace was cooking. "Hello Grace. I had no idea you were here?"

"Where else would I be with my girl hurt."

"Ahh, here of course." She agreed and sat next to Molly, who was drawing. Ava was in a high chair chewing on a hard cookie Grace had made for her. She was teething.

Verity came from the pantry. "How is she dear?"

"Dressing, she will be down shortly. Fin passed out, so she decided to get up."

"Well, good and the hatchlings?"

"Asleep still?"

Molly looked at her mother and asked. *"Me see Auntee June and babbies?"*

"Of course you can. Auntie June will be here soon, and the babies are still sleeping."

"Kay mama."

They all smiled as Grace said. "Did you tell them?"

"No, I decided to wait. Reighn and the others are looking into it, when they know something, we will know. Until then, let's not borrow trouble." At Grace's disapproving look, she sighed. "I will if it becomes necessary, before we have a solution or have no choice. I thought dinner here, what do you think?"

Grace accepted the change of subject if Sage said nothing could be done because they did not have enough information she would leave it alone. So she said. "Excellent, we have just about everything ready, the roasts will be done about seven."

Sage asked. "Verity, will Rene` come here?"

"Of course, June has changed the house into a home, it will hold new memories for him."

"Good, maybe we will tell them after dinner if we know anything or Reighn says we need too."

"Tell who what?" June asked as she entered. "Oh my goodness, what is that divine smell?"

Grace hugged her as she asked. "Hello dear, are you better?"

"Still a little weak, but on my feet."

"Well, good, I have something for you to eat and drink."

Verity hugged her as well. "I am so very pleased you are well. You gave us quite a fright."

June hugged her back, saying. "I am sorry."

"Never mind, do not let it happen again." Admonished Verity.

Grace cautioned her. "You have more to think about now, other than yourself. Fin as well as those precious girls. You cannot afford to be reckless anymore."

Remorseful June told them both. "I know and will not allow it to happen again. I am truly sorry I worried you both."

June kissed Molly, then Ava. "Hello, my girls, did you miss me?"

"*Yes.*" Molly said. "*Isa missed you da most.*"

"I bet you did sweet Molly."

CHAPTER TWELVE:

Fin and June sat huddled together on a sofa dinner had finished ten minutes ago it had been attended by the family minus only a few.

Ella held one of the twins and Scarlett, the other. "So have you chosen names yet?" Grace asked. "I refuse to keep calling my grandchildren, twin or baby."

"Yes, Ma'am we have." June answered, she nudged Fin who smiled. "We have decided, Ella is holding Mirren Everly." Everyone smiled or in the case of the females said. "Aww!"

Fin squeezed June's hand as he said. "Queen Scarlett, you are holding, Breena Dawn."

Again, all the females said. "Aww!"

Verity asked. "Where are the names from?"

Fin smiled as he told her. "Mirren was my mother's name."

"Breena was my choice." June told them. "We decided we would name one each. So I chose Breena because it is of faerie origins and I thought she suited it, like Mirren suits her name."

Fin like the males could not see how the names suited the wrinkled pink haired babies, but no one disputed June's belief.

"Their middle names are courtesy of their Auntie Frankie." June grinned as she nodded to Frankie, who grinned in return as they all looked at her.

"Well, I liked them, they go well with their first names and their last."

Sage said. "They really do."

"Why do you sound surprised?" Frankie asked her.

"No reason. None at all." Sage quickly assured her she had not forgotten Frankie's display of temper in the medical unit. There was general laughter, then talk turned to other matters as people wandered around the room.

Several at one time or another, holding a baby or child in their arms as they talked and looked out at the night. Relaxing in the warmth of a home filled with love.

"Rene ` are you alright?" Charlie asked as she came to him with Justice on her shoulder, who was making baby noises and staring with lavender eyes, which took in everything around him.

"I am." He smiled at the picture she made, a Madonna with child. It was a beautiful memory he would store away, as he would the many he had received since stepping through the front doors of his mother's home.

"Did I tell you my Sire built this cabin for my mother with his own hands?"

"Really, I did not know that, has it always looked like this?"

"More or less, of course we had no indoor plumbing or electricity when I was a boy, it was a vacation home for my mother. We loved being here, my brother and me."

Charlie looked around at the beautiful lounge with its stone fireplace and wooden floors. "You gave it to June?"

Rene ` smiled. "Yes."

He looked at the happy female and Fin, who held her hand like he would never let it go. "Yes, I did, she deserves it, and she loves every bit of this home. Sadly, my brother and I had allowed it to fall into disrepair, we could not face being here, and it weighed heavily on our hearts. It was untouched and unloved until June came and gave it back its heart. She has breathed life back into the very walls and floors and has made it a home for her and her family.

Restored it to its glory and beyond. It is beautiful what she has done here. There is no better tribute to the legacy my mother and father left, they both would be very happy with whom was living here now."

Charlie hugged him. "I believe that, this is a home filled with happiness, you can see how in the future we are going to love coming here."

"Yes, I can." He hugged her back. Verity had been right the memories of the past were still haunting the house, but they were happy memories of a loving family. He thought about all the wonderful times he, Andre` and his parents had spent here and thought of the memories to come. He felt the band around his heart loosen as he looked around him, this felt right, and this would make Andre `as happy as it had made him.

Reighn finally sat beside June and Finlay on the old brown leather couch, he looked at it and ran his hand over a slightly worn patch. "Was this in my old conference room?"

"Yes, do you want it back?" June asked with an edge to her voice.

He could see it in his office it would be good for afternoon naps, but at her look and tone of voice he hurriedly disabused her of that notion and said a silent, fond farewell to the couch. Maybe his Dam could find one for him like this. He turned slightly and quietly said to them both. "Something has come up."

June nodded. "Someone has made a claim for the girls."

He sighed as he hugged her. "Yes, our June there is."

Fin asked. "Pixies?"

"No." Reighn said. "Faeries."

"What... Why... Who?" A confused June asked, like Fin she had assumed the claim would come from the Pixies.

Fin asked. "The paper with details on it, will that help?

Elijah sat opposite them. "Maybe, I have sent it to Keeper and Olinda as well as to my parents, they are researching the Luminia now."

"So why are the faeries claiming them, they do not normally? If they breed true, they will be pixie it seems weird." June asked.

"It does," Elijah agreed, "the claim was placed from a Grove on the other side of the world. No relation to the Sire."

"Can they do that?" Frankie asked as she and Sage came and joined the other couple.

"It would seem so." Scarlett said as she sat on the arm of Elijah's chair.

"It is not common." Elijah pondered out loud. "The fact is they have done so, and we need to figure out why?"

Reighn said. "Someone has decided to start a war."

"Whoa! Big jump there." June almost shouted.

"Hey, how did we get there so fast?" Charlie like June seemed determined to bring them back to the here and now, not leap into war.

"Who and with whom?" Frankie asked, fear shook her voice, she was not very happy about her safe world coming to an end. Fin told her calmly. "With the dragons against the faeries."

"That seems extreme, are you sure?" Sage asked quietly, her eyes on Reighn, who nodded and said. "Simply put, yes. Several poisonings laid at the direct door of the faeries, one attempt to kill or capture the shadow of a dragon. Now the claiming of two hatchlings, which have nothing to do with the Grove claiming them. Harper's near death experience at the hands of faeries."

June bowed her head and thought hard. "Is this an ongoing campaign or is it a result of something else?"

The people in the room stopped talking. It was as though the very air itself waited. Sage swallowed and asked. "What are you thinking?"

June looked up. "Well, was this started before we all came to Dragon's Gap or has it been going on for a while? I mean did it start when the dragons were on their own and dying out or only since we arrived."

"Sela arrived when Edith did and cursed Edith." Olinda said thoughtfully.

"Shit!" Elijah said as he ran his hand around his neck. "I forgot about that, Edith's curse. Scarlett, you always thought Sela was not capable of that spell work?"

"I did, so does the High Queen, we discussed it and researched her history and she was ill equipped to manage such intricate spell work."

"So, that means someone was behind it." Sage tentatively stated.

"Yes it does." Fin said as he stood up and paced. "Let us recap what we know."

"We need white boards." Frankie told them, "To do this in order and not miss anything."

"Third cupboard in my office." June absently said as she sat frowning.

Frankie stood up with Johner and left the lounge as Grace handed out tea and coffee. Shortly they returned with a stand and a white board. Frankie handed Fin the marker. He raised his eyebrows at Reighn. "Oh, go ahead. You have this."

Fin inclined his head in thanks. "Alright let us assume the dragons, and the faeries are being coerced into a war."

He placed both names in the middle of the board. Then, with arrows pointing out from those words, he wrote events and time lines with the help from everyone that were there. June sat and watched the pattern emerge. Claire sat next to her. "Your Fin is very good at this."

June smiled. "It is his gift. It is what makes Fin... Fin."

"Harper honey, are you okay?" Asked Claire of Harper who had not long come in with Ace, they sat together opposite Claire and June. She had her head tipped to the side. "Yep, sure am. What do you guys see when you look at the board?"

"Excuse me?" June asked.

Harper motioned to the board, by now everyone was looking between her and the board. "What I see, is a concerted attack on the dragons."

"As do I." Reighn agreed.

She asked him. "Do you see when it started?"

Fin stood back and surveyed his board studied the diagram on it, he placed his marker on the pivotal point. "Here when this happened." Not one person disagreed.

"When we arrived." Sage stated for everyone.

"Yes, when the dragons opened their doors and minds to the fact shifters could save their race." Grace agreed.

"Who would do this? Fairies. Pixies. Dragons?" June asked.

"All the above." Acknowledged Elijah.

Ace shook his head, leaning forward, his elbows on his thighs.

"No, another, if I am reading this right, we are being played like chess pieces."

"Are you saying the Elementals?" Charlie asked.

"Or the Goddesses." Olinda murmured.

"Ladies please, both those are not possible." Stated Rene`.

"Why? They both place us where they want us. Make things happen when they want. Look at Frankie and me or Olinda and her Goddess. Do not tell me we are not their toys." Grumbled Harper.

"Wow, bitter much?" Charlie asked.

"Seriously, are you going to tell me it didn't happen?"

"Well okay, sure it seems like that. But do you want to take on the Elementals and Goddesses after the week you just had?" Charlie asked with a smirk.

"Point to you." Harper said with a grin.

Charlie said. "Also remember that faerie suggested that there was a male behind her attacks. She implied that he was behind Storms poisoning."

"But can we trust anything she said or did not say?" Asked Scarlett.

"And this is why we never see the whole." Edith said from the doorway as she and Sharm, Keeper and Ella arrived.

Keeper nodded and told them in his quiet way. "We worry about the parts."

"And look to who is to blame, not to why they are doing what they are doing." Sharm said just as quietly.

Storm asked. "Did we forget the unicorns on purpose or just because we forgot?"

Olinda looked at him. "Never even entered my mind. What about you guys?"

Everyone shook their heads as Sage groaned. "No, I will not entertain that idea. I like unicorns."

Olinda grinned as she said. "I like us too. Well, I like ours."

Charlie said. "Ours are faithful and loyal."

Storm said. "So a possibility then?"

Ash agreed. "Definitely."

Olinda sighed. "I put nothing past that old coot!"

"Coot?" Charlie asked with raised eyebrows.

Olinda nodded. "You met him?"

Charlie grimaced as though she had tasted something bad. "True."

Edith looked around. "Well, if we do not figure this out, we are going to be in more trouble. We could get to the point where we do not trust each other." She looked around at each of the people there, her growing family, and said. "I will not allow that to happen."

No one was left in any doubt as to her meaning. Reighn stood with Ava in his arms as he said. "Edee is correct, this is not a way for us to counter this with suspicions and suppositions. That way lies distrust and fractures within our society, within our family. If I am correct, we are under attack. Our very way of life is being corrupted, or at least they, whoever they are, are trying to undermine what we are doing here. I for one will not allow it to continue. So let us all think about who this could be and why?"

"I think the why is fairly obvious." Elijah answered him.

Claire agreed as she said. "To destabilize the coalition between dragons, shifters and faeries."

"Yes, someone wants to be the top dog. Some do not like the dragons being the Elemental's shield." June stated.

Reighn gave Ava to Ace as he moved to the board. "Yes, it seems that June is correct, although knowing is half the battle. Now we can guard against them. Fin, I am asking you to take this over, I understand you are working at broadswords."

Fin shook his head. "My Lord, this is far more important." He looked at June and his daughters. "This affects us all."

Both Storm and Lars agreed, Lars saying. "Anybody got any ideas on who we can get to replace Fin. It will be a hard ask."

Ace said. "Maybe you could recall Hayden." He saw the hopeful look on Clint's face. "It could be the push Master Patrycc needs to allow him to return home."

Reighn nodded. "Agreed, Lars, Storm make it so. Fin, what do you need?"

"An office and my old team, this is what we were good at. I know my team members are not fitting into Dragon's Gap as easily as I had hoped they would, maybe this will help."

"No one likes being cut loose and feeling useless." Verity said, she had not said much until now. "Are there many others that need help to adjust?"

"Not that I know of Lady Verity, and you are right we do not like feeling useless." Fin agreed, he looked at Rene` and Reighn. "We will need him, he has that ability to add two plus two and make five. I feel that this will be required. It is shaping up to be too many pieces of the same puzzle."

Rene` sighed. "I will ask him, maybe we can convince him it is time to come home."

"Who are we talking about now?" Frankie asked of Harper. She looked at her friend and asked in return. "Why the hell would I know?"

"Why the hell don't you?" Frankie snarled back. Much to Harper's amusement, she opened her mouth to retaliate when Ace cut in before the fight grew legs and involved the whole family, which had happened on more than one Sunday family day. "They are talking about Lord Andre`. Lord Rene`s brother."

"Ahh, the black sheep." Frankie nodded, "Well, okay."

All the dragons looked at her. Frankie looked back at them as she asked. "What... say he is not?"

"Well, he is sort of, we just don't refer to him that way." Johner told her, trying to be diplomatic.

Frankie grinned and asked. "Oh, are you scared of him?"

"No, well yes... maybe. He was our trainer as well as our uncle."

All the dragons looked at him with expressions ranging from amusement to smirks. He growled as he scowled at the males there. "As if you are not ambivalent about him as well."

Sage grinning said. "We will still have to have everyone screened."

Rene` looked at Reighn. "I do not like using my gifts for such invasive actions." He held his hand up before Reighn or Sage could speak. "Although, I understand the need. Send them to me."

Frankie asked Reighn. "Do you want Fin's office close to yours, My Lord?"

"I do. Have him, and his team take over the four unused ones at the end of the hall."

"Certainly." Frankie made a note on her tablet. June leaned over and whispered to her. Frankie nodded. "Good idea, never thought of that." She asked her. "You want me to use the connecting room between the conference room and the offices?"

"Yes, it will make a good lounge. It also has an exit to the outside patio which they can use as well."

Frankie was tapping on her tablet. "Okay, will do."

Not much more was added after that, in fact the mood plummeted to one of anger. Reighn let them all talk and get the feelings out, eventually bringing the impromptu meeting to a close as he said. "Okay people we are angry so let's turn that into productivity. We will find who these people are, and we will make it so they can never play this game again. Now let us leave, June and Harper look like they both need a good night sleep."

Everyone said their good nights after they had helped put the kitchen to rights, Fin and June saw them from the house. Finally, they were alone, Fin turned to June. "Go up, I will bring you a glass of wine. We will sit out on the balcony like an old married couple."

June hugged him. "What do you know of old married couples?"

He kissed her cheek. "I read."

"Well, it sounds delightful." She slipped her shoes off and ran up the stairs. Minutes later with the girls sound asleep in their bassinets and just as Fin had said earlier, they were now on the balcony and June was sipping a glass of wine he had brought her.

Fin leaned against the wooden balustrade as he sipped his whiskey and eyed June in her cream colored dress that complimented her delightful hair. "So my shadow, how are you?"

June grinned as she looked into her drink. "I am fine and you?"

"Also fine, quite rested really."

"Well, that is good. I too find I am quite rested."

Fin grinned as he asked. "Not quite the pancake anymore?"

"No, definitely not."

He placed his drink on the table and then leaned a hand on each arm of her chair, caging her in. "What do I have to do to entice you into my arms and eventually our bed?"

June looked up into his eyes and saw his dragon looking out at her. "You could promise me a flight sometime tomorrow?"

"Done!"

"Then you could kiss me..."

He swooped in, and she was dragged into his arms. Her drink slid from her fingers as his lips found hers, cutting off anything more she was going to say.

June had been kissed many times before, never had she been devoured with such finesse. Her heart beat a quick tempo within her chest, causing her mind to blank completely, allowing her wolf to sing her happiness of having her mate with her.

June's fingers found and made short work of his shirt buttons, in seconds her hands found the warm skin of his broad chest, and a groan of pleasure escaped her throat. Fin pulled away as he looked down at his opened shirt, June blinked several times and looked at what her questing fingers had done. "Oh my."

He raised an eyebrow as he said. "Let us go inside, so I too can discover what is hidden under all that delightful material you are wearing."

She grinned, and he glimpsed her wolf in her happy eyes as she reached up and kissed him. He picked her up in arms of steel and with his lips on hers, toed the balcony door closed behind them as he moved unerringly to their bed.

Where they collapsed gently down to discover why bonding was so very important to wolves and dragons

.

CHAPTER THIRTEEN:

In the two days since the revelation that there was a campaign to undermine the dragons and their alliances. Fin had established himself in his offices with his four dragon team. Hines Doyle, Karsen Bryne, Casin Kelly and Lock Walsh, his closest friends.

They had been together for hundreds of years, there was not a one who had not saved or been saved by Fin or each other, time and again. June had been introduced to each of them and had immediately made them uncles to his daughters, sealing their devotion to her and his hatchlings.

The faerie guards Daru Senga and Mercca Ware who had been assigned to protect Prince Tarin, had petitioned to be assigned to Fin's team representing the Faeries. He had spoken to both males and learned they were very good at investigation work. In fact, both males had done just that for the last hundred or so years at their home Grove. It was as a favor to King Elijah that they took on Prince Tarin's protection.

When Jenny Sander's found out about the task force, how she did was still unclear and a puzzle Fin decided he would look into later. She approached Olinda and asked her to intervene on her behalf; she wanted to be part of the unit. Olinda had agreed, especially when Jordan and Ethan Reading had also asked to be included.

He had agreed to their inclusion, so far no word had been received from Rene`s brother Andre` about whether he was going to head up the unit or indeed if he was to return home.

June sat in her office at home reading an official request Fin had just given her, for them both to attend a hearing on the validity of their claim to the twins. "This is not good."

Fin inclined his head, saying. "In one respect it is not, in another we knew it was coming so as it is here, the wondering and worrying will stop."

"You were worrying?"

"Were you not?"

"Well yes, but you seemed so calm about it?"

"I was not, but thank you. It appears my mask of indifference is still in place."

June grinned. "You know I was mocking you, right?"

"Really! I had not noticed." They smiled at each other.

Fin said. "So we have until tomorrow to figure out what we should do."

June grimaced as she leaned back in her chair, throwing the papers onto her desk. "Like what, run?"

Fin nodded, he was deadly serious when he told. "It is an option."

June shook her head, dismissing the idea, even though she knew they could leave and disappear and no one would find them. "No, that is not fair on our families or the girls, especially not on you my love, you have just found Ella. No, we will fight the best fight we can, then we will surrender the girls if needs must."

Fin stilled as his dragon looked out at their shadow, something was wrong, this was not his June. The June he knew challenged males that used swords and guns against her to rescue their daughters. She would never think to give them up now. Speaking carefully, he asked. "You would willingly give the girls up?"

June's heart broke, but she bravely raised her chin and stared him in the eyes. "For the girls, yes."

Fin stood and slowly walked around to her. She stood as well, ready to fight or run, her heart raced in anticipation. She thought she could hear her wolf howling but could not make out what she was saying.

Fin reached out for her and said. "Well, I am sorry, but no. I will never surrender our hatchlings."

June asked stiffly. "Do you think I want too?"

Testing her, he said. "I think you are frightened of what you may do. Therefore, you will do nothing."

June's chin notched up more and she snarled. "You are wrong?"

"Am I? You will hand over our girls, when they and their birth mother sung for you."

June sucked in her breath, her eyes widening as her heart slowed its gallop and she whispered. "Oh, I forgot. How did I forget that? It is so important." Confused eyes stared up at him. "Why did I? Fin my head hurts, what is happening?"

Fin took her hand in his. "Did you forget or was the memory taken from you? I suspect the headache will tell us." He pulled her into his arms as he made calls to Sharm and Rene`.

June asked, her words muffled against his chest. "You mean someone erased it from my memory?"

"Yes little wolf."

"Who would or could do that?" She asked, then she suddenly went cold all over. "Fin I can't feel my wolf."
Tears entered her eyes. "They hobbled her, they made her silent. I have a mind- shield. I practice all the time holding it in place."

He kissed her cheek and whispered in her ear. "Not when you are poisoned my love."

"Bloody hell!" He was pleased to see anger spark as she growled. "Someone will pay for this."

"Yes little wolf they will." Fin agreed as he heard the arrival of the dragons.

Things moved rapidly within seconds of Sharm and Rene` arriving. Reighn flew in with Sage on his back, panicked, she flung herself into the house, screaming for Fin or June. When she reached Fin, he scooped her into his arms and cradled her sobbing against his chest, saying. "Hush sweet Sage, she is well, hush you will hurt your young. Calm now."

Sage gulped in a breath as she tried to talk. "Ri... so... sor... worr..."

He nodded. "I know I really do." Reighn arrived having been delayed by Claire and Lars and took his shadow from Fin and held her close. "My soul, please calm, you will hurt yourself."

"I know... I know." She buried her face into his neck and let the tears fall. "They hurt her again."

Fin agreed. "They did, Lord Rene ` and Sharm are looking at her now. It seems when she was poisoned she was tampered with."

Sage raised her head from Reighn's neck and growled. "Who... who did this?"

Fin smiled. "I think it is time to talk to a certain Faerie Prince."

CHAPTER FOURTEEN:

Prince Tarin sat at the table in the interrogation room and felt the sweat run down his back. Fin sat opposite him, his merciless eyes boring into the brown eyes of the Prince.

Tarin had been summoned from the Groves isolation room where his mother had placed him the day before. Guards put him in silver chains while his parents had stood by impassively, with the Groves Queen and King watching. He was then marched pass them and from the Grove, in front of everyone, and his humiliation did not stop there. Guards then paraded him pass dragons who he was sure laughed at his discomfort. Finally, bringing him into this room where he had been shackled to large bolts on the floor and table.

He was told that the Dragon Lord had asked the Elementals to place spells over the chains and shackles for this exact purpose, and to make escape impossible.

Then once he was placed in this chair and bound by the chains, the dragon known as Finlay Slorah had entered, and they had been sitting like this for ten minutes. Tarin knew because he was counting the minutes, as the numbers on the wall clock flick over.

Finally, he asked, "Why am I here?"

"To answer some questions." Fin answered, his voice calm and bland.

Tarin raised his hands as far as the chain would allow. "In chains like a common criminal?"

Fin leaned back in his chair. "When one behaves or does criminal acts, then one should accept when caught, one will be in chains like any criminal."

Tarin scoffed loudly looking around he knew the mirrored wall was a two way, he had seen enough human cops shows on the screen. "What crime have I committed?"

Fin kicked up one side of his mouth as he answered. "There are several."

Tarin frowned. "Well, what are they?"

"Impatience will not win you any friends here today, Tarin. I am very close to ending your life as it is. So take care."

Outraged Tarin demanded. "For why would you end my life? I have done nothing."

No longer relaxed, Fin stated. "Really and yet you removed memories from my shadow, and created two poisons. One that felled a dragon, and another that felled my shadow. You have consorted with traitors to your realm and mine and you have helped create a spell that caused chaos to friends of mine, resulting in the death of the faerie known as Sela Ouster. You have aligned yourself with those that would kill and enslave shifters and have killed a pixie and faerie, a bonded couple, and tried to kill their young. There is also the matter of trying to instigate a war. None of these are small crimes, I am sure you understand that?" Fin was silent for a moment as he looked down at the opened file in front of him. Finally, he looked up at the worried faerie. "Yes, I think that is all. More crimes may emerge later, but for now we will deal with only these."

Tarin was openly worried now, anyone of those crimes, if proved, would end his life. He swallowed twice and cleared the sudden fear from his throat before he pleaded with Fin.

"You must believe me. I have not done any of those things. I do not know how to make a spell or even what would make a poison, as for consorting with people who are doing those things, that is not my fault. I meet lots of people. I cannot be held accountable for what or who they know. I have no idea about a war. You are crazy, you have the wrong person. I have done none of those things."

"Interesting?" Fin looked down again at the folder in front of him. "I do not believe you and the reason for that, is you did not deny trying to remove June's memories?"

"See, if I was that person you accused me of, I would have said something about that." Tarin's voice took on a soothing dream like cadence.

"Is he trying to beguile him?" June asked as she stood next to Reighn, who smiled as he narrowed his eyes. "It would appear so."

"Amazing." June muttered.

King Gideon looked at his Light. "Did you know he had that ability?"

"No." Queen Isla shook her head. "My dear, I did not, he kept that well-hidden."

"Or it is a recent addition." Elijah looked at the parents of the accused male and felt sympathy stir in his heart for them, to have your only son accused of being a traitor must be terribly hard to swallow.

Tarin's voice rolled over Fin and his dragon said. *Foolish faerie, we should squash him like a bug.*

Fin responded with a laugh. *I find him amusing and stupid. If he is the leader in this endeavour, we will have this wrapped up in no time.*

He is not. Just another puppet that wished to be someone greater.

Sadly, you are correct. I feel for his parents.

As do I.

Tarin softly said to Fin. "You are obviously too close to this. It was your shadow that was affected maybe you should step away. Let someone of rank who will understand me, ask me questions, so I can explain it to them. Obviously you cannot understand simple English, when it is spoken, all this is above your intellect."

Fin sighed loudly. "Are you finished, because it is becoming irritating?"

Tarin's eyes widened. No one had ever dismissed his skill so abruptly before. He was considered above grade, when it came to the art of persuasion, and yet it just slid right off this dragon.

"Sadly for you Tarin your mind tricks will not work on me. I am of rank. I do understand English and worse for you. I do not believe you. Now you may not have realized this, or you did, and in your ignorance thought yourself better than us mere dragons.

Lord Rene ` is a Keeper and I know you know what that is. All fae-rie royalty understand what a Keeper can do. Lord Rene ` searched my shadows mind and found the scar left over by your clumsy at-tempt to remove her memory."

Tarin wiped his face with his chained hands and bluffed as he felt the noose tighten around his neck. "When would I have had the opportunity to do such a thing?"

Fin smiled a showing of his white teeth, for a split second Tarin was sure he saw the dragon in his smile, he swallowed nervously again as Fin said. "We narrowed that down to when you were in the medical unit, when I brought June and the hatchlings back here."

Tarin spread his hands. "There you go, with everyone there as well as my parents, unlikely at best. I doubt I would have been able too."

"I do not, that was when you did so."

Tarin felt fear snake down his spine at the dragon's confident tone. He looked at him and was positive the dragon was playing a game.

Fin said, "Now as for the other charges, instigating a war, poi-son, deaths, spells. I am sure you are not confident or talented enough to do all these by yourself, I want... No, I am sorry, I mis-spoke. I demand the names of your masters and co-conspirators."

"How dare you?" Tarin hissed. "You accuse me of being some-one's puppet?"

Fin looked at the male. "I see."

"What... What do you see, dragon?"

Fin grinned again another slash of white teeth, Tarin was posi-tive his teeth had grown. He swallowed nervously again as Fin said. "I see that being taken for someone's puppet is more upset-ting to you than the actuality of committing so many crimes."

"As it would be to any male." Tarin puffed out his chest as he stated. "I am no one's toy."

Isla and Gideon Ravenswood, parents to Tarin, stood, hands clasping each other's as Isla said hoarsely. "I had no idea, we would never have thought it in a million years. There is no doubt, is there?"

Gideon shook his head. "No my love. No doubt."

June said softly. "I am so very sorry, this must be a nightmare for you. No parent ever suspects their child of such treachery."

They both looked at her and saw the sincerity in her face. Isla said faintly. "No, we did not and thank you my dear."

Scarlett said outraged on her friend's behalf. "Do not take this as your fault, Isla, he is an adult and was raised as his sisters were. There was no reason for him to have done this."

Isla held a sob in as she nodded. "I know Scarlett."

Gideon said, his voice hard with hurt and betrayal. "Look at what he did, with all the opportunities we gave him."

Isla looked at his face and saw the same ravaged expression that she knew would be on hers. "Maybe that was our mistake."

He sighed, as broken hearted as she was. "Maybe, my dear."

Reighn said. "Isla, Gideon, sometimes a bad person is just a bad person. No matter how they were raised or by whom. Remember this as the days go on. At any time he could have come to you, two people who love him and would always help if they could. He chose not to."

Isla smiled weakly. "You are wise, My Lord, and will make a wonderful father. I will hold to your words."

Scarlett said. "It is not that different to what you told me when I was young and Juna left with that male."

Isla nodded. "Oh, I had forgotten that. There was something wrong with him, always was from a little one."

Gideon said softly. "As was Tarin, we ignored and pandered to it. Hid his quirks from ourselves as well as others, but he has that same wrongness inside of him as Definiao Kiltern had. We just hoped it would go away. In that we are very much like Definiao's parents, who were very wrong."

He took Isla in his arms and looked at Reighn. "We will do all we can for you, to halt what he has caused but we cannot witness this. I am sorry for our weakness."

Reighn bowed his head in respect. "There is no weakness here, just heartbroken parents hurting and that my friends, we all understand. Go do what you must, to heal. Know you are always welcomed here at Dragon's Gap and in my territories."

Gideon thanked him as he led his weeping Queen away.

"I hate this, absolutely hate this." Scarlett cried.

"I know my Light, as do we all." Elijah soothed her.

"Tarin, I would never have thought he had the balls for it." Harper said as she entered with Charlie who said. "We waited until the parents left, it seemed wrong to add witnesses to their grief."

"Wow! That was very mature of you." Frankie said as she entered behind them. "Was it Charlie's decision?"

Harper gave her a dirty look as Charlie nodded her head in confirmation. The brief levity helped dispel the despair that had fallen over the room. Charlie stated, "I believe it. Weak chins, and beady eyes. Those that have them, are nasty, evil people." She looked at Reighn. "You sure you don't want me to question him?"

He grinned. "No thank you. I need him alive."

Charlie shrugged. "I don't kill everyone I question."

"Really?" Frankie asked, "Because I am fairly sure the last ones you asked questions of are dead."

Charlie hunched her shoulders a little at the truth of her statement. "Well, yeah but not everyone." She tried defending herself.

Frankie along with everyone else looked at her with varying expression of disbelief on their faces. "I have mellowed. I tell you!"

Harper snorted as Frankie grinned in disbelief. They once more turned to the window in time to hear Fin say.

"Alright, so you take responsibility for all crimes stated, good to know." Then he rose and started to walk from the room. Tarin tried to stand and found he could not. "No... No... No, that is not what I said dragon Fin, you must believe me."

"No faerie Tarin, I do not." Fin remained walking his hand was on the door handle when Tarin screamed and jerked at the chains. "They made me do it!"

Fin halted and turned to him, his face without expression as Tarin sobbed. "I had to do it, I had no choice."

Fin shrugged. "I do not believe you Tarin, you always have a choice. You are a prince you had people to go to, your parents, Queen Scarlett and King Elijah. Your guards, the Dragon Lord. Anyone of these people would have protected and kept you safe." He looked at the male and shook his head. "No, you chose to do this."

"I had no choice." He wept openly as he slumped down into his seat. "I was in deep, they came to me and told me my life was forfeited if I did not comply."

"Who... Who came to you?" Demanded Fin as he stepped closer. Suddenly the room was swamped with power. Fin felt the hairs on the back of his neck rise. June and Reighn along with everyone else watched from the room next door.

"What is that?" June asked as she watched her shadow scan the room.

"Who is that, is a better question?" Harper asked as Reighn walked into the room with Elijah behind him. June and Harper both made to follow, only to be prevented by Charlie, who stood in front of the now closed door.

"Wow! She is fast." June muttered to Harper, who nodded. "Always was."

"Listen up you two. You stay here, no more exciting times for either of you."

"Spoilsport." June murmured to Harper. "Was she always this bossy?"

"Nope, it is a new thing. I think it is having young that does it."

"Tough." Charlie told the two of them. "You can look from here but no going in."

They all turned back to the window. "Hate it when she is right." Harper said to June. They both missed Charlie's smirk to Scarlett and Frankie or Scarlett's wink in reply.

Elijah said to Reighn. "I think My Lord you are under attack, this is Pixie magic. Your magic will not work here, Dragon Lady." He told Sage as she walked in from the hall with blue glowing hands.

Hers may not, mine will! An Elemental said as he appeared. He placed his hands together as if he was in prayer and slowly drew them apart as he did, he revealed two pixies and two faeries standing in the corners of the room.

"Son of a bitch." Harper hissed.

"I second that." Snarled Charlie.

Scarlett mumbled. "Me third it."

The Elemental pointed to a pixie, his voice when he spoke sounded like thunder. *Why are you here?*

A musical voice from the male said. "We are here to make sure the one who has our young return them."

"Lies." Charlie told the others with her in the room.

Liar. The Elemental stated, and the pixie dropped to his knees, tears streaming down his face. His mouth opened in a silent scream.

The Elemental then pointed to the other pixie, a female this time, standing in the opposite corner. *Speak!* Thundered, his voice vibrating the soles of everyone's feet. She looked at the Elemental, then the male on his knees. "We were sent by our Master to kill this one." She indicated Tarin, who screamed at her. "Why? I did everything you asked of me. Everything."

She snarled. "You got caught, fool."

She too dropped to her knees, but there were no tears or silent scream as she clenched her jaw shut.

Harper looked at her sister and the other two. "She is tough."

"Very, but stupid, seriously they want to play here? Foolish." Scarlett shook her head at the stupidity of some.

The Elemental pointed to the faeries. *Which of you will answer?*

A male stepped forward. "I will."

Why are you here?

"To find out who was behind the poisoning."

"Part lie." Charlie murmured.

The Elemental flicked his fingers, and the male dropped to his knees. *You play with words. It annoys me.*

The other person was a female when she came forward, Elijah drew in a sharp breath, they could all see she was half-pixie. She spoke with a lilt that was almost a song.

"Elemental, Dragon Lord, Dragon Lady, cousin. I am here to stop the start of the war."

"Who sent you?" Reighn asked, anger in his voice.

The faerie looked at Elijah, who told her. "You should answer."

"I am an agent for the Elturnian."

Sage said. "I would be impressed if I knew what and who that was."

As would we all! The Elemental said.

Fin told them. "It is the equivalent of our Shields or the human force known as the C.I.A. They investigate more than they assassinate, although they are trained to do both."

The females in the outer room all turned to Charlie, who shrugged. "Never heard of them. That is not to say I have not worked for them but if they are as secretive as they seem to be. I would not have known."

"You know a lot about our agency." The female said to Fin who remained silent, but he did smile a knowing smile.

The Elemental said. *I like our Dragon Lord wish to know why you are here.*

"As I said to stop a war."

But agent, you lie.

Charlie said. "One should never lie to an Elemental. Guess she never got the memo. Scarlett, do you know about these people?"

"Yes, although only in whispers, apparently they are completely autonomous."

"Harmless?" Frankie asked her and almost laughed when she replied.

"Dear Frankie, no. Anything but, all their agents have innate magic and are taught a good deal more, or so I am told. All three of you would make good agents for them and do not be surprised if they do not try to recruit you."

Harper looked speculatively at the pixie behind the glass as she asked Scarlett. "So they recruit others as well as faerie?"

In answer, Scarlett shrugged. "So I have heard." Then placed her finger against her lips in the sign for silence or secret. By now the female was on her knees, panting as she begged the Elemental.

"Please… Please, Eminence. I came because they were here. I followed them."

Thank you, is it in your nature to lie? He asked her.

She drew in deep breaths and nodded, not trusting her voice just then. The Elemental mused. *This seems a waste of your talents?*

Elijah said. "All agents for the Elturnian dedicate their lives to the betterment of all races, or so they say. The actual Elturnian council, consisting of thirteen members at any one time, consider themselves above all others."

The Elemental asked. *All others?*

Elijah bowed his head as he said. "Yes Elemental."

I see, Dragon Lord, I will take these with me and we will learn as much as we can, then send you what is revealed. You may keep the Elturnian agent for now. He turned to the pixie and said. *Do not go far, little agent, we may have a need of you.*

With that, he and the other four people, including Tarin, disappeared. Everyone breathed easier with his leaving. Reighn stared at the female, his mind racing with the implications of her being here. Unlike the others, he, as with Fin, knew quite a lot about the Elturnian, he should, it was his ancestor who originally created the organization. All eyes turned to the female who was climbing to her feet. She made a motion with her hand and looked shocked, and tried again, then said.

"What have you done?"

Sage asked. "Made it so your magic does not work here?"

"Yes." Agitated now, she flicked her hand several times with the same result.

Frankie, Harper and Charlie along with Scarlett entered.

Scarlett asked. "Why are you here, I realized you followed those idiots, but why here?"

The female flicked her hand again, ignoring Scarlett, and asked. "How can you do this? I use Elturnian magic, which is impossible to break or erase?"

She looked genuinely upset. Elijah snapped. "Answer the question now, cousin."

"Because it is my duty." She snapped back. "The leads led here."

Reighn asked. "What is your name?"

He pushed Sage gently into a seat as she answered. "My name is Faline Lightwind."

"Well Elturnian agent Faline you will remain here until you answer all our questions, without magic or communications, unless of course you feel inclined to set it up so I can talk to the head of your agency?"

The female was almost six feet tall with well-defined muscle, if she had wings they were well hidden. Her hair was short and blue as were her eyes, she was not the most beautiful of mixed faerie and pixie, he had ever seen. In fact, Elijah was far more beautiful, but then he was full pixie. Still this female had a certain something that drew the eyes, mystery maybe, Reighn wondered.

She looked at Reighn and smiled a sweet innocent gesture. "It may be possible My Lord to arrange that."

Charlie looked blandly at the female, then Reighn. "She lies."

"As I thought." Reighn dismissed her with a flick of his eyes. "Fin place her in the cells and Charlie take Frankie and Harper with you. Strip search her, and give her something else to wear. Frankie, do the thing we talked about the other day."

"Oh, do you think I am ready?" She asked him with a worried look in her eyes.

He smiled. "More than ready, you can do this. I believe in you sister."

"Oh!" She smiled at his praise, then shimmed her way out of the room with everyone watching her.

Harper scowled. "Dear Goddess, she will be unbearable now. Thanks My Lord."

"Whatever I can do to make your life interesting, sister. I will."

"Bah!" She said as she strode from the room calling out to Frankie.

Leaving Fin and Charlie to escort Faline Lightwind, between them, she said to Reighn just before they passed through the doorway. "You realize this is in violation of the Elturnian code."

Reighn shrugged. "Who? I have no knowledge of who or what that is." His voice hardened. "Because if there was such an organization they would have asked my permission before sending an agent into my territories."

"Faline." Elijah said. "Cousin if you have a way of contacting them, now would be the time to share, do not wait until they come for you. That way ends in blood. You and they do not know who you are dealing with."

She smirked as she said. "Cousin, it is the other way around. Explain to the Dragon Lord who and what we are and how he should be worried for when they do arrive, they will not be gentle."

"Oh sugar." Charlie said, "We don't know the meaning of gentle. Now move your ass."

Fin looked at Reighn. "Tomorrow will be interesting. Where is June?"

"She went with Sage and Scarlett to the hatchlings." Elijah told him.

"How did I miss that?"

"Exactly." Reighn said as he nodded to the female walking next to Charlie. Fin grinned as he dipped his head, saying. "Forewarned is forearmed."

Elijah asked after the door was closed. "What is it Frankie can do?"

"Something extraordinary, she can dampen a whole magical area. We have calculated she can influence five miles at the moment."

Elijah could not quite keep the laugh from his voice as he said. "So Faline, thinks she will be able to communicate once she is in the cells?"

"Yes and she will not."

"Does Frankie have to be close?"

Reighn decided not to tell him everything they had practiced, as he had told Frankie. Sometimes it was better to keep some things close to their chests.

"We will see, but we do not think so." He said instead of telling him that Frankie did not have to be anywhere near the place she affected.

Elijah whistled. "That is amazing."

Reighn rubbed his hands together. "Isn't it, though?"

"Fin knows of this?"

Reighn laughed as he told him. "It was his and Charlie's idea. Now my friend, what do you know about this group known as the Elturnian?"

CHAPTER FIFTEEN:

T hat night they were gathered in the large dining room usually used for Sunday family day. Harper called out. "Quiet down. I have shit to do tonight."

Reighn sighed as he stood at the head of the table. "Thank you Harper."

Harper grinned. "Not a problem, let us just keep on track tonight."

She looked around as Ace said. "Please... Please let us stay on track, the moaning is annoying."

"Whose Harper's?" Storm asked with a wicked look in his eyes.

"No, his." Johner called out, which had everyone busting out a laugh.

Ace grinned as Harper moaned loudly. "See? This is what I mean about staying on track,"

Reighn raised a hand and the talking and laughing slowed to a stop. "Okay, so this is where we are at, for all of you who have not been directly involved. We have created a task force of specialized agents led by Fin. Sire have you spoken to Andre`?"

"I did so, he said he would think on it and let us know."

"Will he help us?"

Rene` smiled. "Of course he will."

Reighn grinned with him. "So as it stands, the task force will be led by Andre` Kingsley. Second will be Finlay Slorah who will take lead until Andre` joins us." There were a few smiles at the mention of Andre`, it seemed he was well liked.

"Fin tell us who is in your unit."

Fin stood and inclined his head. "Good evening everyone, we

are lucky enough to have four of my own team with us. Please stand when I say your name, so everyone can meet you and recognize you. Hines Doyle, Karsen Bryne, Casin Kelly and Lock Walsh, these warriors are former Shields who worked with me." All four stood and nodded to Reighn and Fin then retook their seats, four hardened warriors who looked like they had been front and center of too many battles.

"Daru Senga and Mercca Ware, are as you all know former guards to the Prince. They are first class investigators who were on loan to the Dragon's Gap Grove, but have relocated here permanently. We are lucky enough they have agreed to take the lead with their own teams. We are also fortunate to have Jordan and Ethan Reading. Who, we all know, have unique gifts and are seasoned unicorn warriors. As well as Lady Jenny Sanders, who is well versed in politics? Finally, our ever patient office assistants Lisa Peters and her sister Kera Peters, along with Mike Johns."

Harper looked at the females, she was sure Lisa was one of her rescues. In fact, the more she looked the more positive she was, although she looked very different now. "Lisa is that you?"

Lisa grinned her shiny red hair, and clear blue eyes with a scattering of freckles, belied the sorrowful frightened female Harper had picked up weeks ago. Lisa blushed slightly as she said. "Harper, it is. I know I look different."

"Wow, you do, I didn't recognize you, we should get together later."

Lisa nodded as she retook her seat. Harper smiled as Charlie asked quietly. "One of your rescues?"

"Yes, I wondered what had become of her."

Frankie leaned over and whispered. "She and her sister are doing great, they have helped Claire and me out a few times, and that was why I thought of them for Fin. They are discreet and very good at what they do."

"Thanks Frankie." Harper said quietly.

Frankie whispered back. "It is what I do."

"So now you know my team. Let me tell you what we have learned so far." Fin went on to explain what took place the previous night and what had happened to June. He told them of the agent still in the cells below the castle and who she belonged to. He asked if anyone had dealings with the Elturnian.

It seemed no one had, other than Queen Scarlett and King Elijah. He finished by placing the white board up and explaining the reasoning behind it.

Reighn stood. "So there you have it. What we suspect and what we know. Tomorrow at ten we will be convening court. Two petitions have been brought before the Dragon Lord by a Grove and a Luminia for the return of June and Fin's daughters, Mirren and Breena."

Not one person moved or spoke but the tension in the room ratcheted up, he nodded then said. "As you can imagine, they will not be leaving here with either of them."

Conor Towers, lion, and sheriff of Dragon's Gap said in his slow drawl. "If I was a betting lion, I would bet my life savings, which are considerable?" There were a few laughs as everyone knew the lion gave more away than he kept, to help the people of his new home. "I would say tomorrow at ten would be an ideal time for an attempt to infiltrate Dragon's Gap and kidnap or kill specific targets in the court. Also, tonight would be an ideal time to snatch the agent back I have found organizations like this Elturnian, have only two solutions, for an agent being taken prisoner. Rescue or kill." He smiled when he finished speaking and sat as those around him stared at him, then at Reighn.

"If you were a betting lion?" Charlie said. "That would be what you would bet on."

"Yes." He grinned at her and asked. "What would you bet on?"

"That I would never bet against you."

People laughed at the smug look on the large males face and the shrewd look on Charlies.

Ace agreed with Conor. "He is right."

Reighn nodded, he also agreed. "He is, we have worked out a plan for tomorrow and if Conor and as many of his pride as he can spare would like to be included. We would welcome them."

Conor also nodded. "We would."

Olinda said. "The unicorns are at your disposal, they asked to be included in any plans."

Reighn smiled. "I thank you Conor and you Princess Olinda. Fin, are you commanding?"

"Myself Ace and Conor." They both saluted agreeing to the command.

"Good. Frankie give it out." Reighn ordered.

Frankie stood a bundle of papers in her hands. "These are magical instructions designed by Dragon Lady Sage. Read them, commit them to memory, when you have, the paper will disappear you have until we leave the room to do so."

She passed out the papers to everyone there. Each paper had their duties and where they were meant to be and by what time on it. Reighn said. "Grace, you and your family will have sole custody of all the young. Is that a concern for you?"

"Where?" Ivan asked before Grace could comment.

"Here in the stone apartment, it is reinforced with iron and stone and has magical shielding, all young, yours included, will be there."

Ivan nodded as he looked at his mother and George. Storm told the bear brothers. "Select your people for inside and outside the apartment."

Ivan replied. "We will have them by eight o'clock tonight."

"Good, Keeper and my father will screen them as soon as you have chosen them."

"Done." George agreed.

Reighn turned to Elijah and Scarlett. "You and your Grove may come under attack."

Elijah nodded. "We have sent everyone to the High Queens Grove. Warriors and guards remain only."

Sage asked. "You will stay here tonight?"

"We will thank you."

"Johner, Conor, Storm, the people of Dragons Gap will have to be protected." Reighn ordered.

Conor said. "We have shifters and humans as well as Dragons that have a home they love. No one will willingly give that up to any invaders."

Sage told him. "The young will be brought here along with anyone who wishes to come."

Conor nodded. "We will take the offer for the young. We, the shifters and unicorns can keep everyone else safe."

"You know, the more it looks like we are unprepared the more likely we can lure them in and grab them. A reverse trap." Edith murmured.

Reighn smiled at her as he agreed. "Edee is right, and we will, but I will not sacrifice our people."

Edith agreed, then asked. "No, of course not, but we could ask them if they will help trap these people."

Conor said. "We will, my pride is doing that as we speak."

"Crafty lion." Harper muttered to Charlie who agreed saying. "And smart... very smart."

Sharm said. "I cannot empty out the medical units, as much as I would like too."

Storm told him. "I will have it guarded and brother we can mix in Hunters and Shields with your people. No one will tell the difference. As long as all the young are hidden, it will work."

"They will be brought here." Sage ordered again.

Conor told her. "Dragon Lady they will be here by seven in the morning."

"No, tonight, they will be watching." Ace said. "I would be."

"Agreed, do it like that." Reighn commanded. "So we all know what we are to do. Let us get to it."

"Yes My Lord."

Reighn's commanding voice issued his final orders. "We have eight hours until midnight. We need to have everything and everyone in place by then. Commanders work out a patrol for to-night and the morning."

"Yes, My Lord."

CHAPTER SIXTEEN:

Harper sat in the dark with her back against the stone wall, in the main kitchen of the castle with Ace, she could feel his warm body next to hers. "You know this is the part I hate, the waiting."

"I as well dislike this part."

Harper eyed her shadow. "We could make out to pass the time?"

Ace grinned. "We could, but how would it look to your sister if we allowed our quarry to slip by us?"

Harper scowled at the thought. "Yeah, terrible idea."

Charlie and Storm sat side by side with their backs against the stone wall in the medical unit. Fin had reasoned the French doors would be irresistible to the agents, he believed one would at least try to enter from them. "I am bored. I hate this."

Storm smiled as he softly responded. "I can see that, my love. Maybe we could find something to occupy ourselves with while we wait?"

Shocked he would think of sex now Charlie almost yelled only remembering to lower her voice at the last minute. "Oh, my Goddess we cannot have sex on a stakeout."

Storm eyebrows rose as he heard where her mind had jumped to, which was amusing to him and his dragon.

"I was thinking of playing cards."

Sheepishly Charlie mumbled. "Oh, yeah... we could do that."

"Although your idea has merit..."

Axl and Ark sat together, their backs against the stone wall in Reighn's office. Fin believed the agents would have instructions to search his office, they would not pass up the chance to learn something about the Dragon Lord. Ark had been volunteered by his other brothers to ask Axl what his plans regarding Joy were. "So what's up with you and Joy?"

"It is getting harder to suppress my dragon."

"I feel for you brother. Do you have a plan?"

"No, apart from killing every male here, that is."

Ark smiled. "See, that won't work for me."

Axl rubbed his tired eyes and sighed. "So give me some brotherly advice?"

Ark sucked his breath between his teeth and told him what Rene` had advised to tell him when he asked.

"You know what you have to do. For her, for you, for all us innocent males."

"Shit... that will be so hard to do. I don't know if I am ready yet."

"I get that, but at least you can think about it now. I mean it is that or kill every male here."

"Yeah... yeah, leaving is such sweet sorrow." He misquoted.

"You know, I know you aced English lit. Why do you persist in misquoting everything?"

Axl grinned, knowing how much he annoyed Ark with his bad quotes. "Life is too short to be confined by what was written incorrectly."

Ark sighed and shook his head. "You are a fool, brother."

"A fool in love." Axl sang softly.

"Songs you get right."

Fin and Ash sat together, backs against the stone wall on the level that housed the cells. They were far enough away the agent Faline Lightwind could not hear them. Ash asked. "Are you going to do something about the ones that June tagged?"

Fin nodded. "Of course, as soon as we have this cleared up. Why?"

"Ace came up with a plan to take them out and maybe find out who was behind the attack on the twins parents."

Fin grinned, just a quick slash of white teeth in the dark.

"Please enlighten me and we can see if it meshes with mine."

Conor and his brother Saul sat together, watching the five agents step from behind a curtain of blackness. Barely moving his lips, Saul murmured. "Neat trick!"

"Isn't it, though? Signal Fin."

They watched the five slink on silent feet toward the castle. Conor had guessed correctly they would attempt a rescue tonight. Fin with careful deliberation had targeted this location as their starting point. Of course, how they would get here no one knew or could guess. So Conor sent his pride to circulate within the town while he and Saul elected to remain and watch. They were rewarded just on two o'clock, with the five agent's arrival, and as predicted they split up.

Ace told them earlier at the briefing their leader would assume they would have more of a chance going in alone. It was no easy thing to slip into a castle undetected by the Dragon Lord or dragons, hence the late hour.

So as Conor and Saul watched, Saul signaled Fin, who signaled the teams throughout the castle as well as all the others waiting. He and Ace had placed the teams at what they had determined would be the logical points of entry to capture the invaders. Conor and Saul made their quiet way to where they spied an agent dressed in black from head to toe.

She had not disappeared into the night with the other agents, it appeared something had caught her attention, she was looking up at the battlements where Reighn and Sage stood cloaked in Reighn's magic.

Staring up trying to pierce the darkness, positive something stared down at her she strained to see what it was. Sadly she would never know as Saul and Conor softly padded up behind her and place a small mask over her face.

Inside the attached canister was a potent sleeping gas, Sharm had devised with the help of Sage and a unicorn healer, it induced sleep and lasted for three to four hours. Long enough for the other teams to apprehend their targets and place them all in cells.

Charlie and Storm had no trouble taking care of their target, he never even knew they were there. One moment he was entering the French doors of the medical unit after a cold swim in the moat. The next thing he felt a hand slap a mask over his face, then blackness descended.

Charlie smiled at Storm as he lowered the male to the floor. "That was easy you make a great partner my love."

"So we can play now?"

Charlie eyed her shadow. "We are not talking cards now, are we?"

He smiled like the dragon he was as she grinned like the assassin she was and said. "No, we are not."

Ace and Harper moved at Fin's signal, Harper went into the large walk-in pantry and Ace blended into the shadows in the kitchen, knowing the agent would not turn on the lights. Their wait was rewarded, Harper watched him move stealthily from the door which had barely opened along the wall until the male was nearly at the pantry's entrance. She jumped out and waved her arms around as Ace slid up behind the startled male and slipped the mask over his face. He slumped in his arms as Ace asked. "What was that?"

Harper jumped up on to the counter. "I decided to try a new tactic."

Ace moved to cage her body between his legs and arms. "Why?"

She looped her arms around his neck. "It seemed the thing to do."

"Well, do not do so again, my heart cannot take it."

"Oh... want to make out?"

"Of course."

Axl and Ark were more direct. One minute the female agent was walking down the dark hallway leading to Reighn's office. She felt a wind surround her, suddenly Ark and Axl were on either side of her. "Greetings!" Axl said as the females head turned toward him, astonishment on her face. Ark slapped the mask over her nose and mouth and seconds later she was asleep. "Easy as pie." Axl stated.

Ark snorted in disgust. "Truly. I thought these were some type of hardened agents."

Axl grinned as he hefted the dead weight of the female onto his shoulder. "Well to be fair they have never come up against us or Frankie's non magical abilities before."

"True, we are unique. I wonder if this stuff gives them a headache."

Axl grinned as he offered. "I could try it on you, and you could tell us when you wake up."

"Brother, I am unamused."

Fin and Ash waited, they knew all the other targets had been subdued. Fin had positioned them closest to the cells. Frankie and Johner stood in a room to their left. If the male was able to get pass the dragons. Johner would drop him with a special blow dart made just for this sort of thing by Storm and Sharm.

Frankie tightened her sphere of influence to null the magic's of the male coming stealthily down the hallway. Fin and Ash had moved further along the corridor toward the cell; the agent Faline was incarcerated in.

Fin was fairly sure the male coming toward them was the leader. It was in the careful way he moved and the precision as he scouted the dark hall before advancing. Fin caught sight of Faline moving closer to the bars of the cell. They had deliberately placed her in the cell with a door of bars as opposed to the solid wooden ones.

He and Ash watched the male slip from one patch of darkness to another, when he was almost at the cell, he hissed out. "Faline Lightwind?"

She whispered back. "London Darkchild I cannot believe they sent you?"

"And I cannot believe you got yourself caught."

"Well!" She shrugged. "You have not come up against the Elementals, until you do, keep your comments to yourself. Now get me out."

London leaned against the bars with his senses ranging out around him. He did not realize Frankie's ability was making his senses only read the area an inch or so from his body. Not sensing any danger, London allowed himself to relax and indulge in some teasing.

Faline demanded. "What are you doing? Release me."

London, she knew, could be so annoying, especially if he felt he had the upper hand. It was not often Faline was ever bested by London Darkchild who was an extraordinary human. Descended, if one wanted to believe the rumors from great Native American chieftains, not that he would admit or deny the truth. However, he was an exemplary example of the human race with his long black hair and black eyes, wiry muscled body and sharp intelligent mind. He whispered. "All in good time... all in good time. First though, I wish to know how you were caught."

"Why?"

"It is obvious is it not?" He drawled. "So I do not fall into the same trap of course."

"Huh, you assume it was a trap?"

"Well..."

"Well what? They did not know we were there. We were completely bespelled until the Elemental arrived, then I could not call my magic."

London stood away from the bars he had been leaning against and snapped out. "Say again?"

Faline said with exaggerated patience. "I said no magic. Now get me out of here."

All his cockiness disappeared. "Yes... yes of course." London touched the lock on the door and pushed with his magic, and nothing happened. He tried again, desperate, he looked at Faline who looked back at him with desperation in her eyes. "Try again."

He did, then asked. "What is going on?"

Faline groaned. "Please say you came with a lock pick?"

London shook his head. "Why would I? They are only dragons?"

Her head dropped just as a hand grabbed London's shoulder and another hand slid a mask over his face. "Dragons are sneaky you should remember that?" Fin told Faline as they both watched

Ash allow the male to drop to the floor with a soft groan.

Fin nodded to a stunned Faline, who asked. "You knew?"

"Of course, this is our home. Our Dragon Lord knows whenever a portal is opened. We may be dragons but we have lived a very long time, you may want to remember that, if you survive."

He moved aside as one after the other of his team deposited the members of the Elturnian rescue team into cells on either side of Faline. Ash picked up the one known as London and placed him in the cell with her. She stood back against the wall while the door was opened. She was no fool, there was no way she would try to run, she knew she would only end up dead if she did. After the prisoners were placed in the cells and the teams had dispersed to their beds. Fin looked at Johner and Frankie. "You will be alright here for the night?"

Frankie had elected to remain close to the agents as no one knew what their gifts were. She held tight to her dampening spell. "Yep, Johner said we will be."

Fin told them. "Someone will be down to relieve you in a few hours, so you can change for court. Sleep well, my friends."

"You too." They chorused.

Fin nodded to the agent as she stared at him. "Rest, you will need your wits about you for court tomorrow."

She did not answer him. With one more satisfied look at the cells filled with the sleeping agents. Fin, his hands in the pockets of his jeans, strolled from her view.

Faline slowly sank to the floor, looking at the comatose male in the bed opposite her. Life she feared was about to change forever. The problem, she worried over, would the change be for the better or worse for the Elturnian, and what changes would come for her, if she survived.

CHAPTER SEVENTEEN:

T he next morning June and Fin were up early, neither of them had slept very well after Fin returned to their bed. In truth, there had not been much of the night left.

After they had fed and changed the twins, they wandered into the dining room, where June ate her breakfast or at least tried to. She drank several cups of coffee, she was tired and wired, not a good combination for her or her wolf.

Fin looked at her over the table. "Little wolf, are you with me still?"

June took her eyes off the baby in her arms and Fin could see the wildness in her eyes, he refused to call it crazy and as he smiled at her the look started to fade. Then she took a breath and let it out slowly saying. "I am... I am good. They will be safe. No one will die today, or get hurt and we will be a happy family."

He smiled. "Tall order but doable."

She laughed. "You really are mixing with humans and shifters too much."

He shrugged. "I love the way they express themselves. It is enlightening and confuses the nobles which, as Ace says, is always a bonus."

June shook her head and scolded. "You two really?"

Fin smiled with relief, she was smiling now and relaxing. The feeling of wildness was easing within her as she asked.

"So what is Andre` like?"

Fin thought a moment. "Nothing like Rene` that's for sure. He trained us all at one time or another and there was no one better. He was tough but fair and mostly patient, which for some recruits was a blessing. He, like Storm, does not suffer fools."

"Uhuh! I meant, what does he look like?"

"Why?" He frowned at her question, seeing no reason for it.

"Well, does he looked like Rene`?"

"Oh... I see what you mean. No, he is the light to Rene`s dark."

"Oh different mothers."

Fin smiled at her assumption. "No, just different, they had the same parents. It is just they are very visibly different but very much the same personality."

June looked at him and shook her head; she was still none the wiser as to what Andre` looked like "And you call yourself an investigator."

"I have no idea what you mean?"

"I know." She stood. "Well, we better get ready."

Knock... Knock.

"Who is that?" June asked Fin as he rose with a baby in his arms and went to answer the door. "It should be Harper and Charlie, your escorts for the day."

"My what?" Was all she got out as Harper and Charlie strode in, Harper cut off anymore talking when she asked Fin. "Why are you still here?" And then asked June. "And why are you not dressed?"

She and Charlie were encased in leather pants and tops with long coats. Harper's leathers were a dark blue, and she wore knives strapped to her thighs as opposed to Charlie, who wore black leathers and guns strapped to her thighs.

June asked with a touch of envy. "Wow, you guys look great. Are those outfits specially made?"

"Yeah, Storm and Ace ordered them for us, a while ago." Charlie told her.

"You have guns?" Fin asked June.

She grinned as she said. "You know I do."

"Wear them, and I will also order you a pair of leathers."

June grinned and cheered. "Yippee for me!"

Fin smiled as he handed the baby to Charlie, then shrugged into his sword harness. He, like Harper and Charlie, wore leather armor protection. He kissed June, then said. "Take the girls to the stone apartment. I will see you in the courtroom. Do not do anything rash."

She looked up at him. "I will not, I promise."

He looked down into her eyes and said quietly. "Please do not go anywhere without Harper or Charlie."

"I will not."

He looked at Harper. "Keep Claire safe, you know they will be hunting her first."

Harper nodded as she poured her and Charlie some coffee. "We have them all with Sage, they are safe. Edith is with them as well. What did Claire see?"

"She saw a force of fifty to a hundred. She thinks this is a push, she saw no blood, which she says means they could be scouting."

Charlie grimaced. "It is what I would do to see what our defenses are."

"Yeah, Johner said the same as did Ace." Harper agreed. "It is what I would do too."

"Shit, I hate this." June moaned softly.

"We know, we all do. Stay safe." Fin said as he left.

Charlie nodded to June to hand the baby to Harper so she could shower and change. She told her. "We will get the girls ready."

"Okay, thank you guys."

Harper frowned down at the sleeping baby girl in her arms. "What we do for family."

Within fifteen minutes, the three females and two babies walked swiftly toward the stone apartment. June carried both babies in her arms as Charlie and Harper escorted her.

CHAPTER EIGHTEEN:

C ourt was quiet, even though over a hundred people were present. So many more than June thought would have been there. She walked between Harper and Charlie as they followed Sage, who walked between Claire and Edith.

When they reached Fin, June stood next to him as Harper and Charlie went to where their shadows stood. Edith moved to Sharm, who smiled as she joined him.

Claire moved to sit with Jacks and Sage carried on walking to the podium to stand next to Reighn. Stanvis called the court to order. "Court is closed. Guards seal the room."

They waited while the guards closed and stood in front of the doors. Other guards lined the walls and windows, Stanvis with a nod from Johner called out. "Be seated."

He then took a step back as Lars came forward when everyone had taken a seat, Lars unrolled the scroll and the pageantry was not lost on anyone. "We are here today to determine the validity of the claims from Casadaine Grove and Banatorr Luminia, for the young who have been claimed by Finlay and June Slorah. Please come forward representatives from the Banatorr Luminia."

When two females rose gracefully from their seats and started to move toward the podium, it was easy to see they were pixies. Both were tall and slim and like the twins had long pink hair and green eyes, their skin was golden and shone with vitality. They wore light flowing calf length dresses of reds and yellows. Serenity was the only word June could use to describe them, she nudged Fin. "They look like the girl's mother."

He nodded as he watched the females approach the small witness platform. Reighn stood as they greeted him.

"Greetings Dragon Lord, I am Mauve Bana and this is my sister Neve Bana. We are the cousins of the one named Marria, who passed through the veil of clouds leaving behind two daughters."

The sister named Neve said. "We come in harmony to petition for the offspring."

Reighn inclined his head. "Thank you, we greet you in harmony. I must ask, why do you have a right to the daughters left behind?"

Mauve replied. "They are of our blood, as distant as that is. We feel the connection as faint as it is."

Reighn asked. "Are they the only reasons?"

Mauve asked. "Is there any other than duty?"

Neve stated. "They are pixie therefore they should be raised as pixie."

"Your petition is denied."

Mauve looked at her sister, then asked. "May we have clarity on your decision?"

Reighn waved his hand over to where June sat by Fin. "There is your reason. June Slorah answered the song of the mother and daughters. She suffered life-threatening injuries caused by those that took the lives of the twin's father and mother, to fulfil her promise to the one you call Marria. To bring her daughters to her shadow and Dragon's Gap."

The two females bowed to Reighn, then turned and bowed to June and Fin. "We withdraw our petition, there is no better mother and father for the daughters of Marria than the ones they have now."

June and Fin stood and bowed back. "We thank you."

When Reighn excused them, they silently walked to the door that was opened by a guard and escorted to a portal.

June blew out a breath as Fin murmured. "One down, one to go."

Stanvis called out. "Casadaine Grove, please step forward and state your petition."

Two faeries, male and female, stood and walked to the small

platform. They were dark in coloring, as though they had both been dipped, clothes and all, in chocolate. Both of them bowed to Reighn, then the male introduced himself and the female with him. "Dragon Lord Reighn may I introduce Councilor Carmel Waysong, adviser to Queen Mist Mesa. I am Montel Mesa, brother and adviser to King Palto Mesa of Casadaine Grove."

Reighn inclined his head than asked. "Why has your Grove laid claim to the hatchlings?"

"On behalf of our Queen and King, we bequest the infants be given into our care to be raised as faerie."

Reighn frowned as he said. "Yet you heard the evidence of the call the birth mother made along with the infants to Lady June. You also know of the trials she endured to rescue both young?"

"We did."

"You still wish to proceed?"

"We do."

"Why?"

"I beg your pardon, Dragon Lord."

Sage stood and walked to stand beside Reighn. "I as Dragon Lady ask why? Your petition is frivolous at best. Downright insulting at worse and so I ask why?"

The male inclined his head as the female remained silent. "It has come to our Queen and King's attention you have harbored gray ones. They feel the infants would be unsafe to remain here, due to the inherent dangerous nature of those types of half-breeds."

Harper whispered to Charlie. "Does he mean us?"

"He does."

"Well, that is rude should I explain to him how rude that is?"

Ace said without taking his eyes off the male and female. "Do not yet my soul, let us see what the Dragon Lady does."

"Okay, but any more slights and my feelings will get hurt."

"I am aware."

Sage asked the couple. "Can you explain that, please?"

The female finally spoke, her voice was cultured and very refined. "Dragon Lady, our Queen rightly worries about the infants.

It is a well-known fact that gray ones are notoriously unstable."

Sage raised an eyebrow. "Really? We have not found that. I was assured the information that the gray ones were no longer named as such had been sent to all the Groves by the High Queen and King. Are you saying that your own Groves Queen and King are spreading misinformation or are you implying the High Queen and King are lying?"

The male went a shade darker as the female drew in a sharp breath. Sage tipped her head to the side. "You cannot have it both ways either, your Queen and King are trying to embarrass the High Queen and King by challenging for infants that do not belong to your Grove. Or your royal pair are just misguided and need the High Queen and King to send a recall and close your Grove."

"You have no rights to make such scurrilous suppositions." Stated the female.

"She may not but I do." The High Queen said as she was escorted into the court by her light, King Zale, and followed by Scarlett and Elijah. The faeries dropped to their knees. "High Queen and High King."

Reighn and Sage smiled as Reighn greeted their guests. "Queen Meadow and King Zale, we welcome you to our court."

Meadow smiled as she said. "We thank you Dragon Lord and Lady for allowing us to attend today. If we may, we will take the representatives and their people to your conference room. Where we can discuss this petition and talk about politics and their Queen and King."

"By all means Queen Meadow and please will you and your Light, as well as Queen Scarlett and King Elijah join us for dinner. If Queen Isla and her Light are well enough, please convey our invitation to them as well."

"We would enjoy that very much Lord Reighn, will the one known as Frankie be there?" King Zale asked.

Reighn inclined his head. "I believe she will be."

"Outstanding!" The King said with a decided twinkle in his eyes. "Dragon Lord the petition for the infants is withdrawn."

Stated High Queen Meadow.

"We thank you High Queen."

Meadow bowed her head to Reighn. She looked at the faeries still on their knees. "Rise my people; we will depart. With your permission, Dragon Lord and Lady."

Reighn returned the nod, and she and her Light left the court. The faeries walked toward the door the Queen had arrived by and as the doors opened, Sparrow led a contingent of guards that surrounded the visiting faeries.

Reighn remained standing. "Come forth Finlay Slorah and June Slorah."

They moved to stand in front of Reighn. "Your claim for the two hatchlings known as Breena Dawn and Mirren Everly is granted from this day on, they are yours to love and cherish for as long as you live."

"We thank you Dragon Lord." Fin said as June hugged him, she smiled at Reighn and Sage. "Thank you all."

She looked out at her friends and family. "Everyone, we really do thank you."

Sage called out. "Bonding party next Saturday book babysitters everyone."

There was general laughter as June and Fin went back and sat with everyone else. Reighn let them all talk for a minute, as Sage said. "So Frankie made an impression on the King it seems."

Reighn laughed. "She did, they adore her."

"Is she alright?"

"Apparently, she is thrilled her damping spell works so well." Reighn grinned with pride for Frankie. "On the other hand the agent is furious as well as the other five Fin caught."

"Too bad they broke the rules; they pay the price." Sage looked at her shadow. "You are angry?"

"Very, this is not how the Elturnian are meant to operate."

"Well Fin enjoyed himself, Frankie told me."

Reighn stared out at the smiling male and said. "Practice, he and Ace are very good at this kind of thing. Those agents had no chance. His talent is strategy when he turned his mind to the

Elturnian wishing to rescue the agent. It was he said, a simple matter of logistics."

"Whatever, it seemed to work."

"That it did my love... That it did."

Lars arrived. "My Lord, I know you will be surprised to hear that there is a Councilor from the Elturnian waiting to see you."

Reighn grinned as the court went silent at Lars's announcement. Fin looked at Reighn, who told Sage. "My love please take Mama and sit with the others, let us not allow him too much information."

Sage smiled and agreed, then with Verity left the stage, Rene ` said. "He will know me so I will stay."

When Fin came closer, he said. "As he will know me."

Reighn nodded. "In truth he probably know all of us, but why let him know we suspect?" He then said a little louder. "Alright Lars remain with us, but all others fade into seats and against the walls please."

Which they did swiftly. Fin and Rene ` stood with Reighn and Lars as Johner announced. "They are on their way. Frankie is with them."

Reighn nodded. "Take her Johner and place her with Harper and Charlie. Let's not let them see her."

Johner looked relieved when Frankie slipped through the door ahead of the prisoners and called out. "They are a minute away."

Johner hugged her, she whispered. "I am okay, I promise."

"Good, go sit with Harper and try to look innocent." She laughed up at him, and he could see the tiredness in her eyes. He nodded as she went to where Harper and Charlie sat.

Harper moved over one seat for her. "You look tired, Frankie."

She nodded as she spoke quietly. "It becomes a strain, but it is like a muscle, that just needs strengthening." She smiled at Harper's concerned gaze. "I promise I am alright."

"Good, because the High King and Queen are here and they specifically asked Reighn if you would be having dinner with us and them."

Frankie squealed in delight, Reighn laughed, it looked like

Frankie heard about the King's request. Just then the side door that led to the hall that led to the cells opened and the six Elturnian agents entered.

Faline Lightwind stood in the middle of the other five agents. She was not as defiant Reighn noticed as she had been before, coming to the realization there were others more capable and better equipped than the organization you belong to, must have taken the arrogance from her. Perhaps it was the easy capture of the other five agents the Elturnian had sent to rescue her. They seemed like ordinary people, Reighn even spotted humans in among the faeries, pixies and shifters.

All were beings that could easily slip into Dragon's Gap without raising suspicions. Anger pulsed the room as he thought about how easily they had done so, how many times, he wondered over the years, had they infiltrated his innocent town, and befriended his citizens. His eyes elongated and his voice deepened as his dragon rose to the surface.

Johner opened one of the court doors and a male walked in, he was tall and carried himself with arrogance and self-confidence as some royalty did. Everything, from his bright blue eyes to his handsome face, and slicked-back golden hair. To his black suit and deep blue cloak, said there was not a being in the world that was better or more justified in being alive than him. He was the master of knowledge, of power, no one moved in his sphere of control without his permission.

He was Quin Nightcall, First Councilor of the Elturnian.

He strode into the court as though he owned it, looked around as a sheen of amber covered his blue eyes. He used his power to catalogue and store away the information of the abilities of each person in the room at least that was what was meant to happen. Fortunately, with Frankie there, he was rendered impotent, his abilities nulled.

His blue eyes widened as he once more touched on each person but he could not see the one who had the ability to null his power and worse could not feel the dampening field. So he had no idea how far it covered, was it just confined to the court room or all of the castle? Was it possible it was further? The possibilities fascinated him, how wonderful to bring into his fold, the one with this skill, he almost salivated with anticipation to rub the other councilor's noses in his new acquisition would be amusing.

They had been against the need to send in agents to Dragon's Gap, if they knew he and his hand-picked agents had not only gone against their wishes but also failed, they would surely end his position on the council. If they found out he was actually here, his life would be worthless.

The Elturnian did not suffer fools easily, and as it was turning out, this endeavor was proving to be a foolish mistake.

He should never have gone against the other councilors but when he took this null back with him, as well as the two assassins that lived here, he would again be hailed the only true Elturnian, and they would never question his decisions again.

In that moment he lost control of the rage that was building within him at the audacity of this Dragon Lord to keep these talented people from him especially this null. How dare he hide these treasures from him, it was outrageous.

With enormous strength of will he throttled the rage under control once more as he looked again for some sign of the null. Reighn saw the male glance right over Frankie, as if she was not even there and watched as his eyes almost lit with fire when he saw Charlie and Harper, who gave him back blank looks. Quin lifted his top lip in a quirk of a smile at their expressionless faces, he would change that attitude with training. His eyes lit on Fin where they stopped as a frown marred the perfection of his face.

The male is certainly beautiful. Sage thought. Like a shiny gold coin, he made her powers twitch with irritation. *What is he?* She asked Reighn through their bond.

He replied, not taking his eyes from the male. *No one knows.*

She laughed back at him as she returned. *I bet you do?*

That would be a sure bet.

Sneaky dragon.

Yes, let us hope it is enough.

Quin Nightcall finally strode to where his agents were lined up. Anger made his voice sharper and his eyes bluer as he addressed Reighn.'

"Dragon Lord, I thank you for the invitation to your court." His voice was like a winter's night, rough with a faint accent of something other worldly. It sent shivers down the backs of the shifters and humans alike. Conor Towers, who was in his massive lion form rumbled out a growl that vibrated against the floor and into everyone's bones, causing the hair on the arms of most people there to rise with the knowledge. Danger lurked in the shadows.

Reighn inclined his head, ignoring the grumble from the lion. "I am glad the Elturnian received my invitation. I would have thought the Council would have come themselves and not sent the First Councilor."

Quin bit back the angry retort hovering on his lips. No one sent him anywhere, instead, he bowed his head slightly. "It was deemed unnecessary to trouble the whole council with this matter."

"I see, so I am to assume you are willing to explain your decision?"

"What decision are you referring too?"

"The decision to invade my territories."

Quin spread his hands. "I am here to collect my wayward agents. Not to answer inane questions."

"Take care, Councilor. You are here at my invitation, it does not give you the right to be disrespectful to my court or me."

"A misunderstanding only." Quin hurriedly assured Reighn, he knew it would not do to let those he wished to take with him, see his claws all at once.

"Lie." Charlie said loud enough for all to hear.

Quin spun around but he could not see who had spoken, every face looked only interested, not suspicious. Reighn became tired of the males posturing and demanded. "Explain to me, Quin Nightcall, why I do not end your life and the lives of your agents now. You sent operatives into my territory without my knowledge or permission and sent those same operatives into my house. What part of that is not a violation of our trust?"

"Dragon Lord, we answer to no one. You are treading close to lines of enquiry that you are hardly privileged too."

Reighn's eyes misted over, his dragon raced under his skin, and the room shook with his anger, in that moment the benign ruler had vanished and in his place stood the Dragon Lord whispered about in stories of mayhem and bloodshed. Every dragon there shifted with unease, everyone else held still, not wanting his gaze to find them.

His voice when he spoke was smooth as silk, with an edge of death sliding along the vowels. "When did the credo of the Elturnian change?"

Quin sounded almost bored as he answered. "They are as they always have been."

Reighn's voice became colder. "No, First Councilor, trespassing into a kingdom or world without the consent of the ruling or governing monarchs or government. As far as I know were never in the rules of the Elturnian."

The male said nothing, he stood there knowing he had breached protocol and possibly exposed the Elturnian and some of his confidence seeped from his bearing at Reighn's tone.

Reighn could see when he decided to exert his position once more. It was when his chin lifted and his face became harsh with the stamp of arrogance that seemed to be a habitual expression, the male was out of his depth and if he had looked to his left and seen the look of shame and anger on the faces of his agents. He may have thought twice about what he was about to say but unfortunately his arrogance and belief that the Dragon Lord had no power over him or his role as First Councilor to the Elturnian would be his failing.

Quin stated. "Better to return to your ignorance and leave the Elturnian to our own agendas Dragon Lord, go back to governing your corner of the world and let us look after the rest."

Reighn's dragon entered his voice as he told the councilor. **"Quin you have no idea what you have just unleashed, you had no right to usurp the Elementals or my rule."** Before the male had a chance to speak Reighn's dragon released his voice and he stated

"The Elturnian code is to do no harm, and their mission is to only interject when a governing body calls for help or they have no choice. You had a choice First Councilor, no one was under duress here. Dragon's Gap is not ruled by a tyrant. Dragons are the arm of justice for the Elementals and you should have listened when the Councilors advised you to refrain from sending agents here without my knowledge. In essence, Councilor Quin, you should have talked to me."

"What benefit to the Elturnian are you Dragon Lord." Quin Nightcall sneered as he felt the hand of trepidation slip over his skin.

"As of five hours ago, I am the Elturnian."

"How is this possible, you speak lies?" Quin Nightcall snarled.

"Very easy, I assure you. You and your Councilors made two mistakes. Firstly; my ancestor brought together a specific number of species to watch and help the world when needed. It was not always good, honest people that were given power to rule worlds or countries, so ensuring, no one stepped outside the rules set down by the Goddess. As well as stopping rulers thinking they could become gods unto themselves, and in doing so hurt their populace. He put in place the Elturnian, you First Councilor, have over stepped your own tenets. So as stated in the Elturnian's own laws. I am now required to step in and take over control of the Elturnian.

Your second mistake; was to exclude the Elementals, you, Quin placed the most powerful beings in our universe, if not all universes on bypass. One has to ask. Why you would do this?"

Yes Quin Nightcall, explain to us and our Dragon Lord how it is you think your society has the right to do so. I like my brothers are very interested to know. In the room stood all four Elementals, the one who had spoken stood slightly in front of the others and galaxies swirled in his eyes.

Quin Nightcall could only stand there, shaken from his normal arrogance and unable to utter one word.

Little agent explain, please.

Faline Lightwind swallowed and bowed. "Please Elementals, I

do not know. I am an agent, not a councilor."

But are you not an intelligent agent?

"I am."

We await you.

Faline looked at the Dragon Lord's hard face and swallowed the bile that rose in her throat and started talking.

"From all that I have observed and read, also with a fair amount of supposition. I would say the council felt they had no need to explain their existence to the Elementals. Because they consider themselves long lived and far cleverer, and their reach greater than the Elementals or the Dragon Lord."

As we thought. We are not pleased Dragon Lord.

"As, I am not."

We extracted much from the ones we took with us. A pile of folders appeared in Fin's arms. *You will find everything in there that they knew dragon Fin.*

"We thank you Elementals."

Do with these what you wish, Dragon Lord. We will take the one called London Darkchild, and this one called Faline Lightwind. When we have schooled them, they will return. You may place them as first and second trainers of the new Elturnian society.

"Thank you once more, and I will see to the new society."

Choose your new Councilor wisely.

Then they were gone, taking the two agents with them. Only one Elemental remained, he said. *Dragon Lord, do not take too long. They are an invaluable tool. Erase the corruption within the society as you will.*

Reighn looked over the rest of the stunned agents and Quin Nightcall. "Johner remove them to the cells, they can join the other councilors until I can talk to them. Frankie, you are released with our thanks, the Elementals placed a dampening field around the cells."

"Okay, thank you."

Reighn could hear the relief in her voice. The doors opened, and the guards came in to escort the agents and the bewildered councilor out. An agent asked. "My Lord, will Faline and London be alright?"

Reighn nodded. "Yes, in time they will be better than ever. Go now, I will see you all tomorrow."

"Thank you My Lord." He bowed as the others did except for the councilor who looked as though his world had been removed from under his feet, which it had been, by the time his brain started working again, he would be in the cells with the other councilors answering some hard questions Reighn was sure.

Once they had left the court room, Reighn told the remaining people. "Our Seer was correct, we arrested forty-nine infiltrators. They are being questioned by the Shields now, off world. Thank you everyone for your participation, you all worked well."

There were a few smiles but more worried frowns as they all rose from their chairs. Lars called out as Reighn and Sage left the podium. "Court is dismissed. Go with peace in your hearts."

They all looked at him, some with surprise, and others with amusement. "What? I am trying something new. It was meant to be a nice way of saying, get the hell out."

"Well, it was nice but weird." Harper told him as she stood and stretched, she was still tired from her late night.

"Creepy." Charlie commented.

Olinda smiled at him. "I liked it Lars, it was kinder."

Frankie agreed. "Made me feel all warm inside."

Claire shook her head at him; he raised an eyebrow in return. "You heard them; it made them feel warm."

"And creepy and just plain freaked out." Edith called out, causing several people to laugh.

"None of you have a soul." He retorted as he stormed from the room, which caused more laughter.

Claire declared. "So easy."

"He really is." Reighn agreed with her as Sage hugged him. June was getting hugged by everyone as Fin handed off the folders to his staff.

June finally made it to Reighn and Sage. "Thank you both."

"For what, those hatchlings are yours. June, you were always destined to be their mother." Sage told her softly. "I am proud of you. There was no wolf-crazy."

June blushed. "Well, it was tough there for a minute but my Fin and babies deserve better than wolf-crazy."

"Well, they have that." Reighn assured her.

"Yep," Sage said, "you have finally grown up."

"See that is just mean." June pouted and spoiled it all with a laugh.

.

CHAPTER NINETEEN:

L ater that night Reighn stood on his balcony with a drink in hand as Sage slipped her hands around the hard plains of his body. "What is it?"

"We know the name of the one who has orchestrated the war against us."

"Is it war?"

"It is a kind of war."

"Who is it?"

"The male that enticed Charlie and Harper's mother from her home."

"Oh, my Goddess, does Scarlett know?"

He shook his head. "No, just Fin and I and you now."

"Will you tell Charlie and Harper?" And just like that, he fell in love with her all over again. Asking rather than demanding, he tell them, he knew if he chose not to speak of what he knew to Harper or Charlie, then she would go along with that decision. If he chose to tell the sisters, she would be right by his side. He hugged her to him. "I will have too."

Sage felt a shiver of something roll down her spine as she whispered. "This is bigger than them though, isn't it?"

"Yes, he has spent years planning. Fin says we are playing catch up and we need to do so fast."

Sage held him tighter. "How do we fight someone we cannot see?"

"We fight as we always have, with intelligence and patience."

"But dragons are not alone this time. You have shifters and faeries, all of us to help."

He smiled grimly out at the dark night as he murmured. "And for better or worse we have Andre`."

EPILOGUE:

A portal opened in a small town in the mountains of the Ouachits. Fin read the sign that spanned five feet across. "Mason Town. Population 355. Mayor and owner Jacob Mason. Only Humans allowed within the town limits."

"Seems rude." Johner said as he, Ash, and Fin stepped over the imaginary town line.

Fin looked at him and said. "You sound like Frankie."

"It is catchy but still rude."

"True, we should educate them on this."

Ash advised. "It is our civic duty, to not do so would be just plain rude."

"Are you studying law?" Fin asked the male as he strolled between him and Johner.

Ash grinned. "Olinda likes the law."

Several shadows flew overhead, the dragons had arrived. Fin saw a church like building that seemed to be filled with towns-people. They stopped outside and listened to a male as he thundered about abominations and the power of the sword, he seemed to be getting worked up over what he deemed the corruption of the world because of shifters. He told the congregation that a good shifter was a dead shifter, which was met with loud cheers and foot stomping.

Ash rumbled. "Seems intense."

"I have heard some preachers can be like that." Johner said. "Frankie told me where she came from this was normal on a Sunday."

Fin grunted. "Seems a stupid way to ruin a Sunday."

June stepped in front of the three males. "Hey, are we doing this?"

Fin grinned. "My love, we only awaited you."

"Okay, let's go." With that, she walked up the steps and entered the church and started walking between people, who she was sure had not seen a bath for days, if not weeks, the stench was overpowering.

Her mere presence made people make way for her, or it could have been the three large males holding swords following her. As she walked down the aisle of what had been a church at one time she was unsurprised to see the two males she had tagged standing on the stage. She stopped and called out to the short male who seemed to be preaching to the masses.

"Hey dude, do you remember me?"

The smaller male who she now knew was Jacob Mason stared at her as his face paled. "Go away, you are not allowed here."

The taller male who had been standing behind Jacob, as he loudly spoke of the evils of shifters, stepped forward and stilled on seeing who was with her. June noticed he still needed a bath, his hair, if possible, looked dirtier, and she just stopped the look of distaste crossing her features as he growled out. "Leave unless you brought the abominations back?"

"Nope, I told you, if you thought they were abominations. I would show you some real ones." She smiled at the people there and motioned to the windows. "Look about you preacher."

"I am the mayor and owner of this town."

June shrugged. "Don't care, look up." She told him.

He stayed where he was, Fin thought he probably assumed the stage protected him, he was so very wrong.

Jacob Mason watched as people rose from their seats and looked out the windows, soon the screaming started, and people pushed and ran over each other to leave the building.

Ash was amused, wondering where they thought they could go to be safe, when fire dragons flew, nowhere was safe.

"Foolish humans." Murmured Johner.

Reighn and Ace led twelve dragons in formation over the

town. June grinned at the two males on the stage as she said.

"I did tell you to say your goodbyes to your love ones. I hope you took my advice it's too late now to do so."

She turned and kissed Fin as a portal opened then she stepped through and turning she waved at the males that stood opened mouthed watching her.

Once Fin dismissed the portal, he looked at the fifty or so males gathered on and around the stage, which held the two males June had tagged days before. He asked in a voice that dripped icicles. "Which one of you thought it was a good idea to try to kill my shadow?"

Hours later, Fin held June in his arms as he asked her. "Are you happy little wolf?"

"More than I ever would have believed I could be, if this is a dream. May I never wake up?"

As his lips lowered to hers, he whispered. "This is no dream, my wolf. This is our life."

MAILING LIST

OTHER BOOKS BY L. M. LACEE

Visit my website at www. LMLacee.com and sign up for information, **FREE Promotions** and updates.

Printed in Great Britain
by Amazon